WARNING

This book contains sexually explicit scenes and adult language. It may be considered offensive to some readers. This book is for sale to adults ONLY.

* * * * * * * * * * * * * * * * * *

Please store your files wisely where they cannot be accessed by underage readers.

DISCLAIMER

ISBN-13: 978-1988083018
ISBN-10: 198808301X

Other Books by Darla Dunbar:

<u>The Romeo Alpha BBW Paranormal Shifter Romance Series</u>

Amanda Walker thinks that she has a normal and boring life. That is until after her 24th birthday. Everything changes when she meets the man who says he was supposed to be her husband. Denying everything the man says, she fights him every step of the way. But after he kidnaps her, Amanda discovers that there are some things about her family that her parents kept a secret all these years. Among the history of the family she learns secrets she thought only happened in story books. Can Amanda tell the difference between truth and lies or is she this mysterious woman that holds the key to a legacy?

<u>Romeo Alpha Blood Lines Romance Series</u>

Twenty-four years have passed in relative peace for Amanda and Romeo. They've raised five children into adulthood and are thoroughly enjoying their lives as the Alpha King and Queen of the werewolves. At twenty-four, Sarina is just stepping into her powers and will be ripe for mating when her birthday comes in two weeks. What no one knows is the danger that lurks just outside their tight knit community. Romeo has made peace with the other clans and has enjoyed that peace, but it will all come crashing down around him when his oldest daughter comes of age to take a mate.

<u>The Alpha Feud BBW Paranormal Shifter Romance
Series</u>

Eliza's life consisted of reporting on boring, crowd-pleasing events, like their country livestock fair. With the arrival of two handsome brothers, the lives of Eliza and her best friend, Melissa, are shaken to the core. For Eliza, the arrival of this new man becomes a test of her relationship with her current boyfriend, who she's been happily living with for over six years. Does Hayden, a complete stranger, really wield the power to make Eliza reconsider her relationship with Andrew?

<u>The Alpha Packed BBW Paranormal Shifter
Romance Series</u>

Darlene has led a quiet life since suffering through a terrible break-up. She wants nothing more than to spend her time in front of the TV, away from any sort of trouble. But all that goes down the drain when handsome, rugged and rough Idris comes into her life. He is a werewolf on the lookout for his missing pack leader. Darlene quickly finds herself pulled towards this mysterious man and at the same time finds herself falling deeper and deeper into the world of the supernatural.

<u>The Daemon Paranormal Romance Chronicles</u>

The daemon infighting can only be stopped when a strong leader emerges to calm the different factions. Juno appears to be at the heart of the conflict. Things become complicated when Phoebe and Supay try to negotiate with the siren, Juno. The love triangle among Phoebe, Supay and Apollo become tense when Juno's meddling threatens to destroy any romance that develops.

<u>The Leather Satchel Paranormal Romance Series</u>

Valtina is stuck in Middle World, unable to pass on to The Afterlife. In order to redeem herself from past deeds done, she must help bring romance back into the world and stop The Dark Side from destroying love in its entirety. Following orders issued by Ladaya and armed with a leather satchel filled with the appropriate tools and weapons, Valtina embraces each mission with enthusiasm.

Get the latest update on new releases from the author at:

https://darladunbar.com/newsletter/

This book contains all the stories of the "The Mind Talker Paranormal Romance Series"

Book 1 - Awareness

Ananda discovered that she can read other people's mind when she was 11. It is supposed to be a gift but it's driving her crazy. Lonely and disoriented, Ananda runs off to New York. She thinks that in a city as big as that, there must be someone like her walking around. One day, man's voice calls out to her. The strange thing is that she heard the voice in her mind.

Book 2 - Hunted

Jared's past haunted him and served as a reminder that he can't escape his fate. If he had stopped the boy back then, would his sister still be alive? Jenny was the love of Jared's life until he discovered she was living a double life. Jenny was part of a secret organization that was bent on hunting him.

Book 3 - Heat

Ananda couldn't help herself. Jared's scent just sends her over the edge. No one else understood Ananda's gift... not even her parents. When Jared found Ananda, he explained what her special powers meant. Only certain people acquired the gift of reading minds. Along with that, Ananda was undergoing a maturation process. Every one of her kind will experience it in their 21st year.

Book 4 - Revealed

Jared learns the truth about his dead sister. Ananda had the power to see into his past. She saw what he saw during that fateful day when Jared's sister died. Meanwhile, the truth about Kerri's family is revealed. They are the sole reason why Ananda and her kind are on the endangered list.

Book 5 - Evasion

Ryan is the mystery man who is helping Jared and Ananda to escape to Canada in hopes of evading the organization that is hunting all those with special mind reading powers. Kerri's family is behind the secret organization. Her love for Ryan has forced her to choose between loyalty to family and loyalty to Ryan. Can she be trusted?

The Mind Talker Paranormal Romance Series

Books One to Five

By Darla Dunbar

Copyright Revelry Publishing 2015

Table of Contents

Book One - Awareness

Chapter One

"SO SEXY…"

"God I'd love to do her…"

"I wonder if I could find that outfit in my size…"

Ananda had to fight laughter, curling an errant lock of dark auburn hair around her finger as she fought through the crowd of people around her. Laughing for no reason, at least none that could be seen by the general population, is typically frowned upon and usually makes finding friends much more difficult. This she had learned the hard way thanks to the cruelty of middle school students and their need to be popular. Still, it never ceased to surprise her how many inane thoughts humans regularly had running through their minds. Sometimes, Ananda had to totally isolate herself in order to get a moment's rest, particularly when surrounded by the chatter from all directions. Her honey-colored eyes flitted back and forth as she scanned the mass of people around her, thoughts flying into her mind in rapid succession.

It wasn't like Ananda couldn't turn it off, her ability to hear other people's thoughts. When she was younger, it was definitely more difficult to sift through the roiling voices and images that seemed to seep into her head with little direction or effort. At first when her ability manifested at the tender age of eleven, Ananda was terrified as were her parents, who were ignorant of such abilities. Her older brother Ryan had been a source of strength and stability for her as the family went from one psychologist to another attempting to find a reason or cure for the 'voices' Ananda claimed to hear. It was he, who helped her find a center in order to control the flow of voices until they were barely more than a brush against her mind. Ryan's move across the country for school was rough though manageable for Ananda as she began to explore the range of her ability and discover the fun she could have with it. Her moral compass wasn't as low as some, so she didn't use it for anything that would get her ahead academically, but she did use it to benefit herself and those she loved.

"Ananda, over here!"

Refocusing on the crowd around her, Ananda spotted one of the few people she could actually call a friend. Kerri wasn't what anyone would call quiet. Her small stature and pixie-like features made it seem as if she could be blown away by a single puff of air, but her exuberant personality and sharp, sometimes biting, use of sarcasm made her seem larger than her thin frame. Bright red hair the color of the sunset and eyes that seemed to change color depending on her mood completed the full package that was Kerri Donahue. However, it wasn't just Kerri's larger-than-life personality that drew Ananda in, it was more of what Kerri didn't exude. Her mind was quiet.

No matter how intently Ananda poked and prodded, she could only get a faint hum and vague feelings from her friend's mind. Rather than being unnerved by that, Ananda felt a sense of relief at finally finding one person who didn't give her a headache just by being around so often. Even with her brother Ryan, Ananda had to occasionally leave in order to calm her own mind and get some relief from his mind's 'voice.' The fact that Kerri seemed oblivious to how special she was sometimes made Ananda pause and wonder if she was the only one out there with a strange ability. Was there someone out there like Professor X who was searching for people like her? Was there a way to find others? Or did she spend way too much time reading comic books and hoping that some parts of those stories were influenced by actual facts?

Chapter Two

In the nine years since Ananda discovered her ability to read minds, not once had she ever come across anyone who seemed to be able to do the same. She had tried going to palm readers and calling so-called psychics, but so far they had all been scams. Their own minds would betray their lack of abilities sometimes before Ananda had even handed over her money. She had decided upon going to NYU with the vague hope that in a city as crowded as New York, there would be at least one other person who shared in her ability that she could commiserate with. After two years of hoping and searching, she had grown discouraged and until meeting Kerri, Ananda had even considered moving back home to Phoenix and abandoning her search altogether. Meeting the other girl had been soothing to her soul and Ananda felt renewed enough to continue her search for others like her; she had even decided to expand her search overseas.

As soon as Ananda was close enough, Kerri linked their arms beaming up at her with a beatific smile. Ananda couldn't hear anything, but she could sense a general feeling of comfort emanating from the shorter girl.

"So I was thinking. After this farce of a homecoming game," Kerri sneered at the direction of the scoreboard, "Perhaps we should hit up the quad and do a little man-hunting. It's been way too long since I got any action and I know for a fact that you haven't had anything between your legs that didn't require batteries for far longer."

Ananda couldn't help her snort of laughter. It was true that she had been experiencing a bit of a dry spell for the past few months though she wasn't a prude by any means. Sex had always been fun, even though most people seemed to have the same mantra running through their heads.

"Don't stop…more…"

"Feels so good…"

"Yes…"

There were a few times where she was surprised by thoughts of violence, though they had never physically manifested with her, thankfully. And still there were rare moments when it seemed as if the other person could read Ananda's mind. She would be thinking about a move one of her previous partners had done and the new one would do it. Or if she were enjoying one particular position and her partner was about to change it, they would jerk as if shocked by something and change their mind. Sometimes Ananda wondered if perhaps she had other powers and abilities that she was just unaware of.

"…just better than any guy I've ever met!" Kerri finished with a high little squeal bringing Ananda's attention back to their conversation.

"Who?"

Kerri paused to look at her friend. "Did you hear anything I just said?"

"I heard the part about sex and my vibrator and then something about more sex…possibly with a guy…" Ananda shrugged as her voice trailed off. Truthfully, she didn't really want to know what her friend was talking about. Sex for her had gotten stale and boring and until she meets someone amazing, Ananda doubted she would feel inclined to do something about her lack of sexual partners for the past few months. "Honestly, I just haven't been in the mood for anything with anyone." She smiled and leaned into Kerri, bumping their shoulders together. "I'll just have to live vicariously through you and perhaps sleep with my ear against the wall."

Ananda smiled as she watched her friend laugh uproariously.

"I'll try to be extra noisy just for you my friend. But first I need to scope out the competition." Kerri turned to survey the crowd leaving Ananda free to scan the voices coming at her from all sides.

"So fake. I can't believe she did that!"

"If he doesn't propose I'm leaving!"

"I really hate her…"

"…Ananda…"

Startled, Ananda jerked in place as though she were slapped. She could hear Kerri still discussing the merits of one guy over another, but the sound of that deep voice saying her name had her attention. It wasn't the first time she had heard her name in someone's thoughts, but it was the first time that it felt as if it were meant for her alone. Trying not to be obvious, Ananda scanned the crowd hoping to spot the person behind the thought. Everywhere she saw people utterly focused on the game; no one so much as glanced in her direction.

"…and that guy looks like a serial killer or child molester or something. Like, didn't anyone ever tell him that those mustaches are just not attractive? I mean think about that in bed, the whole…"

"…I know you can hear me…Ananda…"

It was unnerving. As much as Ananda had desired to find someone like her, now that the moment was here she found herself wanting to run. Something inside of her was repulsed by the idea of someone else being able to see inside of her mind and she quickly put up a barrier in her mind. She could feel Kerri tense up and wondered again if her friend had abilities she just wasn't yet aware of.

"Are you okay, Ana?" The concern in Kerri's voice was so thick it was almost physical. Ananda felt the desire to wrap herself in it like a child burrowing into his mother for comfort.

"I…" She could feel another brush against her mind as if someone were asking for permission to enter. "I'm not feeling very well. I think I want to head back to the apartment." Unhooking her arm, Ananda forced herself to appear calm so as not to draw any unwanted attention to herself. It was difficult with the overwhelming amount of concern her friend was radiating. It hadn't been this hard for Ananda to block out the feelings of others in a long time and if not for Kerri's naivety she might have actually snapped at the girl.

"What's wrong? Should I go with you?" Kerri reached out in an attempt to grab Ananda's wrist, but she paused as if sensing that somehow it would be the wrong move to make. Once again, Kerri's attentiveness the minute Ananda's demeanor changes was surprising. Only Ryan had ever been able to read Ananda once she learned to block her own thoughts and feelings. Normally she would feel grateful that her friend was so attentive, but at this moment, it just made her feel even more cornered, as if she were the prey in a fight for survival.

"Ananda…relax…" That voice in her mind, she couldn't be completely sure but it sounded so familiar to her. Almost as if she had heard it in a dream. She tried to calm her mind while continuing to discreetly scan her surroundings. She was a bit worried that if the guy was good enough to penetrate her mind's defenses, that he would be more than skilled enough to hide the fact that he was broadcasting his thoughts to her in the first place.

Turning back to Kerri, Ananda forced a semi-sincere smile on her face in an attempt to placate her friend's concern. "Nah, I'm fine. I'm just going to go back and put on some PJs and relax with a book…non-academic, I promise." Ananda was quick to add after seeing the thunderous look on Kerri's face.

"Good! I've been telling you for months that you've been working too hard. Go relax, take a bubble bath or something." Laughing, Kerri pushed Ananda back towards the way she came. Her kaleidoscope eyes still had lingering concern, but she gave a small smile for reassurance. Ananda stopped for a moment and really looked at her friend. For some reason she felt as if this would be the last time she would be able to see her friend for a long while, and for a moment she contemplated ignoring the voice in her head and wrapping herself in the cloak of safety Kerri always seemed to exude.

"You're right," Ananda replied, pausing to pull her friend into a much-needed embrace. She let the scent of Kerri's strawberry shampoo wash over her as if committing it to memory. "I love you, Ker." Pulling away quickly, Ananda hurried off, without a backward glance. She knew if she looked back at her friend, she would be unable to do anything but clutch at the smaller girl. Perhaps if she knew what was waiting for her, she may have looked back after all.

The trek back across campus was a little disconcerting for Ananda. On one hand, there were still people milling about, laughing about the lousy game or enjoying a drink or two with friends. A few times Ananda was stopped by someone she knew from class or the few nights she deigned to do anything other than study in the library. The entire journey back to her apartment, she couldn't quite shake the feeling of being watched, as if someone was just waiting to materialize from the shadows. The feeling put her on the edge and more than once, Ananda found herself peering intently into the shadows, listening for the voice which had so unnerved her previously. Was the person still at the game? Did she know them? Surely she didn't just imagine everything; she was gifted, not crazy. But why after all this time was the person coming out to her now? And why did the voice sound so damn familiar? These were thoughts and questions that could only be answered when she found the person who called to her.

Chapter Three

Ananda crossed the street as her apartment came into view. Out of habit, she glanced up at the window of the apartment she and Kerri shared and was alarmed to see it illuminated. She could have sworn that they turned out all of the lights before they left. Had Kerri decided to come home early as well? Slowing her walk, Ananda reached out with her mind, confusion spiking when she brushed across something cold and wholly unfamiliar. Just then she could see a figure moving in the hallway, almost into view. Something inside her began to freeze at the thought that the person in her apartment was there for a far more sinister reason than just talking, and she found herself frozen in place with panic. The figure moved even closer to the window and Ananda knew that if she didn't get a hold of herself then she would easily be spotted standing alone on the sidewalk.

"Move!"

The thought burst through her mind's defenses as one hand gripped her wrist and another covered her wide stretched mouth. She was dragged into a narrow alley between two buildings and found herself struggling against someone with far more strength than her 120-pound frame possessed.

"Breathe…quiet. We don't want to be felt, otherwise we're both dead. Understood?"

The person behind her tightened their grip and Ananda nodded once briefly to convey that she understood. Despite being pulled into an alley by a stranger whose size and stature far dwarfed her own, Ananda felt surprisingly calm. She did what the stranger said and focused on breathing slowly and silently through her nose. She was intrigued to find a scent, cloying and sweet like honey, that seemed to be emanating from somewhere in their vicinity. An answering scent, musky with a citrus tint, seemed to unfurl around her and she jolted when she realized that the smell was coming from the person still holding her so closely in the middle of a dark alley. She wondered if the man knew his scent was so enticing and if it was a brand of cologne that she could buy in order to have it covering her always.

As if sensing the direction her thoughts had gone in and how little of a flight risk Ananda really was, the man behind her slowly peeled his hand away from her mouth and brought it down to clutch at her hip. A shiver of electricity seemed to travel from the stranger's fingers directly into Ananda's suddenly oversensitive skin, and she could feel him tense.

"Stop it…"

Despite not being able to see the man, Ananda could tell that he was scowling, gaze sharp on the back of her neck even as his errant fingers began softly stroking the sensitive skin of her hip. Just that little contact seemed to ignite a flood of pleasure in Ananda's body, the strength of which she had never before felt. It was as if her body had been put on pause until this very moment, a fateful meeting.

"Wait."

Turning her head slightly, Ananda caught a small glimpse of the man behind the haunting voice. She was momentarily taken aback by the sharp cut of cheekbones that trickled down into a sculpted jaw covered with dark, day-old stubble. The top half of his face was still shadowed, but she knew his attention was still focused on the apartment light that shouldn't be on. Trying to focus on the situation at hand, Ananda turned her gaze back to the direction of her apartment. She couldn't see the window from where they were hidden, but she somehow knew that even the slightest movement would give up their location in the dark. She forced herself to mentally relax and focused on making her mind as clear and see-through as possible.

"Good, you're doing good…"

The praise from the dark stranger made Ananda practically purr, and she tried to distract her mind from the desire to turn around and grasp that chin before attacking what was sure to be a sinfully decadent mouth. No one's inner voice could be that sensual without there being some outward evidence of it. The man's scent was still wrapped around her and without thinking, she took a long drag in as if to embed it into her nostrils permanently. She wondered how she smelled to the man after being surrounded by so many people earlier. As if reading her thoughts, the man's head came forward and he nosed behind the shell of her ear. Ananda could feel the hair on the back of her neck stirring with each breath the man took and she hoped that he found her scent as mesmerizing and intriguing as she found his. For some reason, she wasn't concerned about why she could so clearly pick out the aroma of the still silent man over the pungent smell of trash.

"Who are you?" Ananda whispered as quietly as she could without drawing attention to anyone who happened to walk by. It wouldn't necessarily be a good thing to get caught in an alley at night with a strange man who may or may not be a serial killer. Though the fact that all he had really done was hold her and sniff behind her ear made Ananda less inclined to think of the man as a killer. Then again, wasn't it always the quiet ones you had to look out for? "Are you going to like, kidnap me and cut me into little pieces or something?"

The man tensed for a moment before his shoulders began shaking up and down. His breath huffed out beside Ananda's ear and she could tell the man was laughing at her. Before she could get worked up enough to demand answers, she was jolted by the man's gravelly voice.

"Jared."

Chapter Four

Swallowing reflexively, Ananda tried not to tremble. "Jared. Okay. Great name. So, how about my other question?" The man stopped his quiet laughter and once again tensed behind her. "Are you planning on killing me?"

"…No."

Relaxing, Ananda tried again to see the man's face fully. "So what are you going to do with me then? Why are you here? Who the hell is in my apartment? Why is someone…" Ananda trailed off from her incessant questioning as a familiar hum brushed against her mind. "Kerri!" Jerking her gaze back to the street, Ananda almost threw herself out of the alley at the sight of her friend walking up to their apartment building. If not for Jared's sturdy grip she would have been halfway down the sidewalk before consciously considering her actions.

"Quiet!" Jared hissed tightening his hold once again. The hand that had been gripping her hip once again came up to muffle the enraged sounds tumbling from Ananda's mouth as she struggled to reach her friend. She was terrified. There was an unknown intruder in their apartment whose very aura was enough to scare Ananda without even trying, and her unsuspecting friend was being led like a lamb to the slaughter.

"Calm down and stay quiet!" Jared's inner voice was practically growling at her with impatience, the fury of it enough to bring tears to Ananda's eyes. "I will keep your friend safe. Just trust me and calm the fuck down!" Swallowing down a sob, Ananda forced her eyes to follow her best friend's path and was startled to see the lithe girl pause in the middle of the sidewalk with a look of barely contained confusion. It seemed as if Kerri couldn't make up her mind what to do for a moment before nodding and turning back the way she came. Ananda's state of shock was so great that she didn't realize Jared had begun leading her back towards a car he had stashed on the other side of the alley. It wasn't until they were moving steadily away from her apartment building that Ananda seemed to remember she had been practically kidnapped by some unknown stranger, and she turned to finally take in the man.

His day-old stubble looked just as inky black as it had in the alley and Ananda could see he had thick eyebrows of the same midnight hue. His hair was lush and thick with a slight curl that made her want to run her hands through to feel if it was as soft as it appeared. Broad muscular shoulders were barely even contained in a tight black Henley that screamed criminal, but those weren't even his best feature. No, that would be his eyes, ice blue and glinting like diamonds. Ananda could tell that this man had been through some unimaginable situations though he looked like he was roughly around her own age. She wondered what more he knew about these abilities and how he had managed to get Kerri to turn from danger with just a thought. Her mind was such a rolling mess of confusion and half-formed questions that their abrupt pull into a motel off the side of the highway barely made a blip on her mind's radar until she found herself in an unfamiliar room perched on the edge of a really uncomfortable mattress.

Ananda blinked slowly up at Jared who stood in front of a window peering into the darkness of the night as if looking for something. "What is going on Jared? Why did you bring me here and who are we running from?" Ananda was almost startled by how breathless she sounded, but the still present scent of the man in front of her was still wreaking havoc on her senses. Surely the man could tell the effect he was having on her?

"And why do you smell so good?"

Jared jolted away from the window and fixed an intense stare on Ananda. "I smell good? You have no idea how difficult it was for me to hold still in that alley." He walked slowly over to the bed until he was so close that Ananda was forced to tilt her head up at an awkward angle to maintain eye contact. The temperature in the room seemed to jump a couple of degrees and Ananda could feel her skin begin to moisten with sweat. Unconsciously, she licked her lips and her eyes widened as she saw piercing blue eyes hone in on that small unconscious movement. Without thinking, Ananda reached up and ran a soft finger across Jared's brow before placing the offending digit in her mouth and closing her eyes with a groan. How was it possible for sweat to taste so sweet? She could hear Jared's breathing become labored and she shivered with the knowledge that she was affecting him as much as she herself was affected.

When Ananda opened her eyes, Jared was gazing down at her face, positioned like he was expecting her to go running and screaming into the night. Strangely enough, she had no such thoughts other than getting everything she could from this man, right there and then. Scooting back on the bed, Ananda flung herself back hitting the two small pillows that they had before pushing them to the side. She wiggled a little to get comfortable while raising both arms over her head and arching her back. It was the first time she had consciously used her physical body only to entice another person. The way Jared's eyes seemed to darken as they trailed down her prone body made her think that perhaps she should try it more often.

Jared's gaze zeroed in on the small sliver of skin where her shirt had been lifted with her arm movement. Stalking her onto the bed, he leaned his face down to nuzzle and mouth at that stretch of skin igniting nerves in Ananda's body that she had previously been wholly unaware of. She had been turned on ever since first being pulled into the alley and her core was starting to ache with the need to be taken and repeatedly filled. Never before had a partner solicited such a response from her as if their bodies were being magnetically pulled to one another. It didn't look as if Jared was much better off, a sizeable bulge clearly visible in the dark jeans he was wearing. Still, he hadn't moved beyond nuzzling her stomach and Ananda was beginning to wonder if perhaps she was just dreaming. "Jared?"

The man finally looked up, eyes burning with so much clear desire and such hunger that Ananda couldn't stop the whine that pushed past her throat. Never had a man looked at her with so much need and it made her question all of the sexual encounters she had had before. Slowly as if not to startle her, Jared moved closer, eyes still fastened to the reddened skin of her lips. Ananda leaned up those last few inches in order to bring their mouths together in their first kiss.

What started out as a slow exploration quickly turned into a torrid affair of bitten lips and thrusting tongues. Ananda couldn't stop the sounds tumbling from her lips as she gasped and sucked on Jared's upper lip. His hands were like hot brands running up and down the sides of her body, shirt being pushed further and further up with each pass until the bulk of it was tucked into her under arm. Sinful fingers slid up to brush maddeningly soft and then skin-scorching harder circles against her upturned nipples. Ananda's bra was pushed underneath her ample bosom as Jared's lips migrated down to suck and nip at first one and then the other in quick succession. Ananda found she could do little more than arch and gasp as her nerves came alive, goosebumps popping up like wildfire on her overheated skin. She squirmed until she got one of her legs free in order to plant one foot on the mattress, knees spread wide enough for Jared to settle between. She could feel the hard heat of his manhood pushing against the fabric of her shorts and Ananda found herself angry at the thought of anything between them.

"Off," she said hoarsely, and shoved at Jared's shirt until he leaned away from her sensitized nipples in order to pull the offending garment off. The moment he was free, he dove down, tongue tangling with hers in an obscene parody of what their bodies would soon be doing. It was like Jared would die if he didn't get more of her mouth and tongue. Ananda was finding herself distracted by the breadth of Jared's back, the heated warmth of his skin and the way he shuddered when she scratched her nails down his spine. Suddenly Ananda knew what that cloying honey sweet scent was. It was her!

Her body had been reacting to Jared's since the moment they came in contact and his had been responding in turn. Now the air was full of the smell of pheromones released with every bump and grind of their bodies. Despite this, Ananda had no intention of stopping until she was sated. She bucked her hips up into his in an effort to show him she was ready to get down to the main event. Detaching her hands from his wide back, Ananda slid them down to grasp at the buttons to Jared's jeans. He made a hoarse noise in her ear as he leaned back letting her peal the zipper down and pull out his quickly hardening cock. The sight of him made her mouth water with the desire to feel that heavy heat on her tongue. She got a few enthusiastic strokes in before Jared was twisting out of her grasp and backing up and away from the bed. He kicked off his jeans and underwear and Ananda couldn't help but gaze hungrily at the man in all his toned naked glory.

Sculpted abs and pecs led down to a happy trail that made Ananda's fingers itch to tangle with. Jared's cock was a thing of beauty, hard and weeping slightly with the evidence of his desire. He gave her a moment to stare before reaching for her again to help Ananda out of her shorts. When she made a move to remove her panties he stopped her by simply angling them out of the way, eyes focused on her hidden depths.

"How far do you want this to go Ana?" It was the first thing either of them had said in a while, and Ananda startled, not expecting the question or the familiar nickname. Jared was sitting back balanced on his haunches and Ananda suddenly knew without a doubt that if she said it, Jared would be content with just kissing and frottage for the night. Leaning up to wrap her arm around his neck, Ananda pulled the man on top of her and reached down with the other in order to line his cock up with her pulsating core.

"Everything. Give me everything, Jared."

The sound of his name must have been more than the man could handle, because without another word he drove into her, slickened walls ensuring his smooth entry. Though it had been months since Ananda had last been with anyone, the abrupt and quick entry gave her nothing but toe curling pleasure and she didn't think twice about wrapping her legs around Jared's torso. She could feel the muscles in his back as he surged into her over and over again, the sound of skin meeting startlingly loud in the otherwise quiet room. Their lips met, though it was less of a kiss and more of breathing in one another's air as gasps and moans were shared back and forth. Ananda could feel her body clenching with the need for release and she gripped Jared's ass in an attempt to push him deeper inside of her. Sweat slickened her brow as she tossed her head back and forth in an effort to stave off her release. As if knowing her predicament, Jared pushed himself even harder, cock brushing against her core and setting off an explosion of fireworks behind her eyelids. But it was inevitable that the end would be reached and as she heard his familiar voice inside of her head, Ananda's body snapped into an arch, every muscle tightening with release.

"Come for me…"

Distantly Ananda could hear Jared's groan as her body pushed him into his own climax, but she could do little more than breathe as her vision faded to black.

To be continued in Book 2

Book Two - Hunted

Chapter One

WAKING UP was an experience for Jared. It had been years since he had felt an inkling of the comfort that is sleeping wrapped around someone he didn't have to worry about stabbing him in the back. It had been months since he last let his guard down enough to be intimate with anyone other than himself. And yet this girl, someone who had never even been properly informed of what she was, had somehow blown clear past all of his defenses before he even realized they were down. It gave him an uneasy feeling the fact that he responded to her so quickly. He had thought himself incapable of feeling anything for another person other than hate and mistrust after all he had been through.

Jared's life wasn't rough in the beginning. He grew up in a normal family household, with normal parents, a normal older sister and a normal dog. Overall his early life was completely and utterly normal. And then came puberty.

His freshman year of high school brought the normal bouts of acne and anger indicative of a boy on the journey of becoming a man. Being the nerd that he originally was, he had read every article and book on the subject that he could get his grubby little hands on, including some not so hidden Playboys that his dad kept stashed in a cooler in the garage. Everything that he had been experiencing was so tragically normal that it was almost a relief when he started hearing the voices. At first he had thought himself crazy, mad like the hatter from Alice and Wonderland, until the voices began to sound familiar. He could make out his sister's voice, shrill and lively even when muted. Then it was his parents. Soon he was hearing every thought contained in his high school and he realized what real crazy was.

It was a chilly day in November, the day before Thanksgiving break, ironically, when one of his classmates, a boy who had been picked on and bullied for years and who Jared had been close acquaintances with moving in similar social circles, decided that he couldn't handle the pressure anymore. Jared had known that the boy, Kevin, was unstable just by listening to his rather disturbing thoughts day in and day out. He could hear the boy plotting something big, something that would stop his never-ending pain. Jared had known all this and yet he had done nothing. He was still getting a handle on control and though the boy's thoughts were filled with darkness, on the outside he appeared put together and in control. Jared feared that at best no one would believe him and at worst he'd put himself in harm's way if Kevin decided to take out his anger on him. So Jared stayed quiet, never even telling his sister who was in the year above him, his concerns.

Jared had been sitting out on the lacrosse field where he normally took his lunch so he could avoid any awkwardness in the school cafeteria. His sister had often offered him a seat with her friends, but he usually turned her down in favor of his solo spot. It wasn't that he was anti-social, it was just that he knew one day he would grow into his looks and be, if not attractive, then at least average. However, he didn't want to sit for forty-five minutes and hear his sister's harpy friends with their high-pitched inner voices squawking and gushing over it. He thought that people who said women mature faster than men were horribly misinformed and probably home-schooled.

It was for this very reason that Jared heard rather than saw the commotion that happened without any warning. One minute he was biting into an apple, geometry book balanced on one knee, and the next he found himself sprawled on his side with his ears ringing as his lungs fought to pull in air. All around he could see bits of rock and drywall lying beside him and for one minute he wondered if he was dreaming. Slowly he started to make out the sounds of screams over his groans as he pushed his body up into a seated position. The scene that unfolded before him was straight out of a war movie. The school was entirely engulfed by flames and one of the cafeteria walls was completely missing. Some students were running out of side entrances while others were already huddled across the street, loudly wailing and clutching one another for comfort. All around Jared could hear the flood of thoughts running wild.

"Oh my God! It's just like in a movie!"

"What's happening?"

"My classmates are dead. I saw a dead body…oh God, I saw a dead body!"

Covering his ears to try to block out the voices, Jared stood in an attempt to get as far away from the building as possible until he heard the one voice he had always been careful to block out.

"Jared…safe…hurts…"

"Sofie!" The sound of his sister's inner voice, so weak and in pain sparked Jared into action. He moved to go towards the cafeteria, into the area where he knew his sister always sat when four strong arms grabbed him and pulled him away from the scene. Screaming and yelling, he fought to free himself and free his sister from the crumbling debris, but the hands were too strong for him. Soon all he could do was shake as he stood across the road and watched firefighters and emergency officers fighting to put out the blaze. Some students were being carried out in stretchers or on the backs of others. Jared watched closely, desperately hoping to see his sister's long midnight black hair among those being brought over. He watched until the blaze was out and emergency workers began searching for bodies. He watched until his parents pulled up, his mother screaming and beating the chest of the officer appointed to the task of delivering the bad news. He watched his father slump to the ground, head clutched in his meaty hands as he sobbed for the first time Jared had ever seen. He watched it all and he knew.

This was all his fault.

His sister's death was one of many that day. Out of the three-hundred students in the cafeteria that day only twenty managed to make it out alive. Kevin had apparently made the decision to take out his tormenters as well as himself and had situated himself as close to that table as possible before detonating his bomb, a bomb he had strapped to himself and had hidden under his clothes. The official report was that the boy had been planning this for a long while and had found instructions on the internet for how to build a bomb out of normal every day materials. It also had a quote from Kevin's mother stating that her son had been harassed for years by his classmates and that he had recently began 'hearing voices.' That last statement stopped Jared cold. It was then that he realized the deaths of over two hundred of his classmates was and would forever be on his conscience. If only he had stopped and talked to Kevin, let him know he wasn't alone in the world of voices then maybe this tragedy never would have occurred. Maybe they could have learned to help each other and maybe Sofie would still be alive to pester Jared into dressing better or telling him how handsome he would be when he got older. Maybe she wouldn't be rotting in the ground while their parents' marriage fell apart. Her death meant the death of their family and the beginning of their father's love of alcohol. Jared retreated even further into himself, switching schools when his mother moved them across town and making minimal effort to get to know anyone. He graduated with honors, moved across country to attend Columbia, and as Sofie and her friends predicted, he grew very well into his looks. Working out 5-6 times a week gave him the relief he needed by pushing his body until the point of exhaustion. The fortuitous side effect of such hard work was an impressive physique. Suddenly he went from a nobody to a somebody that girls and guys alike wanted to sleep with.

Chapter Two

He had been frequenting the library looking for books and articles about people exhibiting extra abilities when he really should have been working on his literature paper when he first met Jenny. Unlike some of the girls he had previously gone for, she seemed to be more mature and put together. Her thoughts were a gentle hum in his mind rather than the chaotic ramblings he was privy to when interacting with other girls on campus. He could only really catch a word or maybe an errant feeling and rather than being wary of that, he was intrigued. It had been a long time since he found anyone out of the ordinary and he was curious to learn more about her.

It had taken him weeks to get her to actually talk to him thanks to his impressive reputation around campus for being a 'one and done' type of guy. However, once they began talking he discovered that they had quite a bit in common. She was double majoring in neuroscience and pre-law and believed that the next step of evolution would not be one of physical means but rather mental. Her ideas of the next step of evolution were fascinating to Jared and he wondered if perhaps she had abilities of her own. Then came the day she finally let down her defenses and it happened.

They had been having an invigorating discussion on what would be the next step after the discovery of evolved humans when Jared leaned across the couch and kissed Jenny. Initially she didn't respond and Jared began to worry that he had misread the situation, until the moment he felt her fingers tangle in his hair angling his head so that their lips slotted together perfectly. The moment their tongues touched he knew that he wouldn't be sleeping around with anyone else. Something about her called to him and his body responded faster than it ever had before. Before long he was straining uncomfortably in his jeans and he could feel the fabric beginning to soak through thanks to his weeping member. Making an executive decision, Jared hooked his hands under Jenny's knees and stood up. She wrapped her legs around his waist as he carried her into the single bedroom in his apartment.

Laying her down and removing himself from her warmth was a test in patience and they both laughed at the clumsiness of their hands as they quickly stripped one another of all clothing. Once Jenny had him stripped, she moved faster than he thought she could until all he could feel was the pleasurable warmth of her sinfully wicked mouth.

"God Jenny, your mouth," he groaned, fingers tracing the edge of her mouth where it met his pulsing cock. What little she couldn't fit into her mouth was being squeezed and massaged by her small but confident hands. Jared could feel tremors running up and down his spine as he fought not to let go too quickly. He could feel every ridge on the roof of her mouth as her head bobbed torturously slowly up and down his shaft. The slurping sounds alone nearly made Jared lose his head as he stared at Jenny's hollowed out cheeks. He could see saliva and his own slick dripping steadily down the girl's chin as she made humming noises to express her enjoyment. The vibrations set off nerve endings and had fireworks appearing in front of Jared's eyes until he forced himself to pull Jenny up in order to chase the taste of his own wetness from the heat of her mouth.

Jenny broke the kiss with a moan and pushed Jared to lay flat on the bed. "Lie back and relax baby." She positioned herself about Jared's lap, her moist core dangerously close to his uncovered cock. Jared had never slept with anyone without some form of contraception and for some reason unknown to him he felt no desire to push the issue. He already knew he'd be with this woman until she pushed him away and so he was ready to take whatever she wanted to give.

The feeling of her moist heated walls against the skin of his shaft was damn near overwhelming and Jared could do little more than grip the sheet with one hand and Jenny's hip with the other.

"Jared baby, you feel so good." Jenny rocked slowly up and down only pulling off slightly before re-seating herself firmly with a little swivel in her hip. "Feel me up so nice. Your big hard cock pushing inside of me."

Jared groaned, the sound of sweet Jenny talking dirty to him was enough to push him right back to that edge. "Fuck Jen. Too good I'm gonna shoot already."

"Then maybe we should slow down, do something else?" Jenny abruptly moved off Jared and laid on her back beside him with her knees pointed out. "Maybe I want a little of that oral pleasure, hmm?"

"Oh yeah Jen?" Jared quickly flipped over and slid down so that his hips were under Jenny's thighs. "You want me to taste you, drink you until you've got nothing left to give?" Using a finger, Jared traced up and down the woman's sensitive folds, smiling at the shiver that ran down her body. He could see her shiny hole already slightly wider thanks to his cock having been in there only moments before. Moving his face closer, Jared breathed in deep and was startled to find that Jenny didn't smell like much of anything down there. It wasn't good or bad, just completely non-existent. He wasn't sure what that was supposed to mean as he didn't usually offer this to any of his female partners, but he did think that women were supposed to have a certain kind of smell. When Jenny moaned though and her body pumped out a bit more slick, all thoughts of the strangeness left Jared and he was once again focused on the gorgeous writhing creature before him.

Putting his lips to her folds, Jared let his tongue dart out and push slowly into her hidden depths. Her taste was a bit like her scent in that it was barely there or non-existent. Still, he wanted to try hard to make it good for her. He opened her carefully with his fingers while flicking his tongue rapidly in an obscene parody of what his still hard cock wanted to do to her. He could hear soft gasps and moans leaking from her mouth and he reveled in being able to make her feel overcome with pleasure. Before long he could feel a subtle shift in her body before her walls contracted and she was flung headfirst into ecstasy.

Jared slowly withdrew his tongue and leaned up to cover Jenny's body with his own. When he tried to kiss her, she was quick to turn her head however, and didn't seem interested in tasting herself on Jared's lips. He chalked it up to personal preference before reaching down to slide himself in deep. He could feel their hips meet and he paused to enjoy the silkiness of her channel. Soon though nature made him move as his instinct to bury himself in her took control. The sound of skin slapping together was almost deafening, Jenny throwing her head back to voice her pleasure to the world as Jared buried his grunts and groans into the dampness of her neck. Her nails scratched lines on his shoulder blades and that little bit of pain is what sent him tumbling over the edge, hips speeding up as his body pumped his release into Jenny's moist cavern. Both of them were panting and out of breath, loathe to move and break the afterglow of their first coupling. Soon enough Jared disentangled himself from the bed and moved to the bathroom to get a wet cloth in order to clean them up. He tried not to think too hard after seeing his release leaking down Jenny's thighs and instead curled up beside the already dozing woman.

The next few weeks were nothing short of amazing for Jared. He had a woman who was beautiful, intelligent and loved having sex whenever and wherever the mood struck her. She had once cornered him in a section of the library that was seldom frequented in order to suck him off. One minute Jared was laughing and playing along and the next he was stuffing a fist in his mouth to keep from shouting the place down as Jenny showed that she had mastered the art of deepthroating. The force with which he came was terrifyingly amazing and his brain was so shot he didn't notice that Jenny hadn't swallowed but instead had spit into a jar.

Then there was the time Jenny had handcuffed him to the bed, put a bandana over his eyes and then ridden Jared for close to an hour. Every time Jenny could feel him getting close she would stop moving, instead just holding Jared's hard member inside of her. He felt a little uncomfortable at first with the idea of being tied down and blinded, but he pushed away the feeling and concentrated on pushing himself to climax. During this time he could never quite get a read on Jenny's thoughts. He could feel that she was pleased with herself but it was still mostly silence from her thoughts. If he hadn't been so enamored of her, maybe he would have taken the time to wonder about the silence he got from her mind; how someone without abilities was able to shield herself from him with little to no effort. But he was in love and he thought those feelings were reciprocated until the day came that pushed him onto the path of searching for people like him and running from those who hunted him.

"Jen I don't think this is a good idea," Jared whispered as he ducked under a wooden beam. He was clutching a flashlight as he followed Jenny into an abandoned building. He wasn't completely sure how she convinced him to sneak into the building. It was only that Jenny had told him she wanted to explore the old asylum because of its history of inhumane treatments. She wanted to see if she could find any files that detailed the happenings.

"Don't worry! This place has been abandoned for decades now. No one is going to come in and kick us out or anything." Jenny stopped and leaned heavily against Jared's side, fingertips trailing down his chest and toying with the edge of his jeans. Just that little motion caused a flare of heat to rush through his body and he knew his cheeks must be slightly tinted pink with his arousal. For the past few months his arousal had been hitting hard and heavy to the point that he swore he could actually smell his body releasing citrusy smelling pheromones. He wondered if Jenny could smell them as she never commented or even seemed to be aware of it.

"I'm not worried about that," Jared lied easily. "It just doesn't seem like this place is all that safe and I don't want you to get hurt..." Feeling slightly foolish, Jared let his voice trail off into silence and continued to follow Jenny deeper into the building while alarm bells went off in his head. Something just wasn't right about what they were doing.

"Jen seriously, I don't think we should be doing this." Jared glanced around the darkened room, eyes straining against what meager light they had to see if anything was out of place.

"You're right about that, but it's too late for you now." Suddenly pain bloomed hot and bright across Jared's temple as the world went pitch black around him.

When Jared awoke, he was chained against the wall and he could feel blood dripping down his scalp. He was startled to see Jenny sitting calmly in front of him, not a scratch on her but with a smirk he had never seen her wear before.

"Jen?"

"Not quite love." Standing, the woman who had been his lover for the past six months looked at him with barely contained triumph and disgust. With a jolt Jared realized that all of the moments they spent together, all of the memories and future plans had been nothing but lies. He should have questioned himself harder as to why he couldn't hear Jenny's thoughts. Why all he had ever gotten were vague emotions and sporadic words. Why after all of the time he had spent in the library he had never seen her there before the day they met. His blind, naïve trust had made him an easy catch and what's more, he had willingly run headlong into it with his desire to be loved. He could feel something within him hardening and he knew then that feelings of love and devotion were nothing more than a weakness, a tool others could use against you to get what they want.

"Who are you?" Jared asked, none of the traces of who he used to be evident in his voice. He felt a sick thrill when the smirk on the woman's face slipped just a little. He could almost smell the nervousness starting to radiate from her. "Why did you bring me here? Why play this sick game with me?" His voice rising, Jared could feel a tickle starting at the base of his skull. It was almost like an insistent itch that he longed to scratch. Jenny's smirk fell completely and she was left looking distinctly unprepared for the questions Jared was asking. Her confusion only fueled Jared's rage and heaved himself off the floor to stand fully in front of her. "Answer my fucking questions!"

Rather than surprise her, his command seemed to relax the woman whose face went from surprise to blank as if she were unaware of herself.

"My name is Jodie Hamilton." Her voice was almost monotone, devoid of any inflection. Jared stared for a moment, mystified by the sudden change in the woman's demeanor.

"Good. Why did you bring me here?" Arms straining, Jared fought to break the handcuffs that bound him to the wall while keeping his eyes locked on the woman in front of him.

"I brought you for my boss. He ordered you to be contained in a secure location until his arrival." The information was making Jared's head spin. From what it sounded like, his seduction and abduction had been premeditated before he and Jenny had ever met. It might even be possible that her whole reason for even coming to the college was to find Jared and set him up. The memories of them spending so many nights twined together in the throes of what Jared had thought was mutual passion made him want to vomit.

Looking up at the woman who had lied to him for months gave Jared the strength and sheer anger to not break down. "Who is your boss? What does he want with me?"

"I don't know. He never shares that much information with me. I'm supposed to find you, seduce you and deliver you to the drop off point for extraction." Jared could see Jenny's body beginning to shake as if she were trying to fight off whatever hold he had on her. What little light her lamp provided showed that her skin was ashen gray and dotted with beads of sweat. He knew he needed to push hard and fast if he wanted to get out before whatever Calvary she had called actually arrived.

"Fine," Jared all but growled, irritated by the skin of his wrists as the cuffs bit into them. Eyes snapping up to Jenny's, he summoned every bit of a commanding tone he could scrounge. "Uncuff me." He could see Jenny's hand snap up and then hesitate as if she were unsure whether or not that was a good idea. His eyes narrowed in fury as what little patience he had ran out. "NOW!"

To his surprise and amazement, Jenny hurried to fulfill his command, bringing out the keys and unlocking his handcuffs. The moment Jared was free he grabbed the woman by the back of the neck, barely able to contain his fury as he stared into the eyes of the woman he thought he would one day marry.

"I want you to forget you ever met me. Forget you were ever supposed to find me. Leave this building and never think of me again." Jared reluctantly let go and watched as Jenny turned and left the room. That was the last time he dared to imagine himself having a normal life.

Chapter Three

In the months and years after, Jared practiced using his newfound gift of persuasion. He still had numerous liaisons with women, but now he made sure that they would forget him after, and he was always careful to use protection. He switched his major to computer science and began studying and honing skills he needed to obtain information on who or what might be hunting him and others like him. It was completely by accident that he had run into Ananda a few months ago. The minute he felt her mind touch his it was as if time itself stopped. Not even with Jenny had he ever felt this way and the idea of an even greater loss of control with another person made him wish for some harm to befall the girl. She looked to be a few years younger than him with thick wavy auburn hair and striking golden eyes. A trick of the light almost made her eyes seem to glow with a fire that threatened to scorch him. And as if all of those things hadn't been attractive enough, there was her scent, honey sweet and trailing behind her as if by command. She seemed to be completely unaware of the eyes that were drawn to her in her wake as she laughed with a smaller waif-like girl with blazing red hair and eyes that seemed to swirl with magic. It was worrying that all he could get from the smaller girl was a faint hum and a feeling of contentment, but he ignored the tightening of his chest in favor of moving along down his path.

Despite his desire to ignore the girl, he found himself growing more and more intrigued. Who was she? Did she know about her abilities? Did her friend know? All these questions and more were running through his brain and he pledged to find answers to them. It was scarily easy to obtain information about her from the registrar. He knew that her name was Ananda Reyes and that she lived in the student apartments just on the edge of campus with the red-headed girl. He knew she was aware of her abilities and he'd seen her use them in ways that were eerily similar to his own.

He told himself that he was just looking out for her in a brotherly way, making sure she didn't get into too much trouble. And yet every time he saw her go home with some boy who wasn't him, a part of him burned bright with rage. It wasn't until the moment that he was pressed against her in the alley that he realized just how far he had fallen. The sight of his old lover, Jenny, walking into that apartment had spurred him into action. With Ananda unaware of what awaited her immediate future, Jared knew his fate was sealed. He would go to the ends of the Earth and back just to make sure this girl was safe.

Though he had pledged to himself to keep Ananda safe, he was unprepared for the effect her scent would have on him. He found himself hardening fast, and even though they were surrounded by the stench of trash and waste, the desire to bend her over and have her right then and there was damn near overwhelming. Only the thought of being caught by whoever had been hunting him kept him from doing something incredibly stupid in the alley. No, he will save it for later.

In retrospect, being contained in a small space with the object of your desire spilling fresh pheromones everywhere probably wasn't the best idea he had ever had. If he had been a better man, he would have gotten two separate rooms and retreated to take care of his sexual frustration alone. He may have been able to control himself if not for the innocent thought that drifted his way.

"Why do you smell so good?"

The realization that Ananda could smell him as much as he could smell her broke whatever control Jared thought he had and before he could regain his senses he found himself balls deep, buried in a warmth that threatened to break the tenuous hold he had on his feelings. Every thrust felt like a cleansing and every gasp and moan like the words of an angel. Afterwards as he lay beside her sleeping body, Jared's eyes took in everything about her from the point of her nose to the ample swelling of her bosom. Somehow in the midst of so much chaos and pain, he had managed to find the woman who would complete him. He didn't know how he knew, but he just knew. And now that he had her wrapped safely in his arms, he dared anyone to try to come and rip them apart.

He knew that this battle wasn't over; it hadn't even truly begun. For some reason there were people out there hunting people like him and Ananda, and Jared would not rest until he could be sure that the woman asleep in his arms would be safe.

To be continued in Book 3

Book Three - Heat

Chapter One

TYPICALLY, on a normal day, Ananda woke up securely warm and cocooned in the down-filled blankets of her bed. The window over her bed had no blinds, only sheer curtains that fully allowed the rising sun to shine brightly, illuminating the room and waking her gradually. What she did not normally wake up to is her skin overwrought with sensitive nerves, itchiness demanding her attention, and skin feeling one degree away from boiling. Slitting her eyes open, Ananda could see moonlight seeping through a crack in curtains that absolutely did not belong to her, creating random shadow patterns on the wall that did nothing to calm the frantic beating of her heart. If not for the familiar arm stretched out around her waist, she would have jerked out of bed. As it was she simply gazed around while letting her mind catch up to the situation.

Shifting slightly, Ananda was unpleasantly surprised when a bolt of pain shot down her spine. "Ow ow, fuck ow! What the hell did you do to me?!"

"…Nothing that you didn't ask for."

The unexpected answer pushed a small huff of laughter between Ananda's lips until her breath was coming out in wheezing gasps. She could feel herself beginning to panic and who could blame her? Her skin felt like it was on fire, she was in bed with a man she met barely a day ago and she was running from some unknown entity that broke into the house she shared with a best friend who she was afraid she'd either never see again or would only hear about on the news. All things considered, panicking was the tamest thing she could be doing at this point when compared to the alternatives such as running screaming into oncoming traffic.

Ananda considered calling her parents and then quickly pushed that thought from her mind. All she needed was for them to once again think that she was crazy when she explained about hearing other people's voices and apparently finding someone who shared that same gift. Not to mention having to explain to them that she was currently shacked up with said person in a slightly sleazy hotel room after having explosive sex that left her catatonic for…

"How long have I been out?" Ananda would have been surprised by the breathy quality of her voice if she weren't still trying to gain control of her body and regulate her breathing. The hand that had been resting on her stomach was now moving softly in a circle that, amazingly, was helping her regain her sense of calm. That musky, citrusy scent was back and curling softly about her, somehow cooling the heat that settled right underneath her skin. She could feel the aches from their previous bedroom activities diminishing until all she felt was a dull buzz. "God that's like catnip or something…" Her voice trailed off into a satisfied gasp. The hand on her stomach paused for a moment but once again continued after she whimpered softly.

"You've only been asleep for maybe an hour," Jared's deep voice rumbled. Ananda could feel the vibrations travel down her back and she shifted back into the man's warmth more fully until she could hardly tell where he began and she ended. She once again thought about calling someone, particularly Kerri, at least to check and see if her friend was okay. Then again, she knew that if she called then her friend would without a doubt come to wherever the hell they were without a second's hesitation. Ananda wasn't too keen on having her friend burst in while she was still in the thralls of whatever heat wave her body had decided to fling itself into.

So she relaxed back into Jared's stable arms once again closing her eyes and relaxing into the silence. Strangely she felt no need to talk or fill the room with any sound other than their soft breaths. Despite the abrupt situation that she somehow landed in, Ananda felt more comfortable with Jared than she ever had with anyone else. She could feel his thoughts slowly unfurling and yet she felt no need to push to read into them more clearly. It wasn't that she was uninterested, more that she felt he would let her in on them when needed. Until then she was content to leave him to his own private musings while taking whatever comfort he was willing to give her. The fire that had burned bright under her skin had tempered itself and though she still felt a bit antsy, overall it was manageable.

Ananda fell back into a slight doze, waking slightly when she felt the arm slide away from her waist and the bed shift with motion.

"Jared?" She intoned sleepily, turning slightly in order to peer at the man over her shoulder. Her body no longer ached and instead she felt almost energized, a warm buzz of contentment just under skin. She caught a glimpse of the man's broad muscular back before the form turned and she was looking up into those amazingly blue eyes that seemed to glow with some unnamed emotion always present right underneath the surface. Jared peered down at her for a few moments before he leaned over to kiss Ananda deeply. She reached up to card her fingers through the rasp of his stubble enjoying the scratchiness against the skin of her fingertips. When he pulled back there was a ghost of a smile lingering on the man's lips and Ananda settled back into the pillow with a small smile of her own. Somehow she knew that it was imperative to get as much sleep as possible for now and so she closed her eyes as Jared moved to the bathroom shutting the door softly behind him.

The next time Ananda woke up was less than pleasant. The agonizing itchiness was back as was the molten fire burning underneath her skin. She made a short relieved sound as she scratched her nails down the skin of her arm, a choked noise escaping her throat as she attempted and failed to quell the sensation of her skin burning from the inside out. Ananda's back arched as a sharp sensation of arousal flared from deep inside of her.

"What the hell…" she panted. Never before had she felt such a strong sensation. Truly looking around for the first time, Ananda realized with dismay that she was alone in the hotel room. Glancing at the side table, she saw a phone with a note stuck to it. Without thinking she grabbed it, dialing the number that Jared left for her

to use. With every unanswered ring, Ananda could feel
her mind growing more and more alarmed, the panic
that had been earlier pushed back threatening to make a
reappearance.

"Yeah?" Jared finally answered, annoyance clear in
his voice. It took a few tries before Ananda could push
back the panic in order to get her voice to work.

"Jared…" she moaned as another jolt of arousal
nearly made her double over. "Something's wrong. I
feel so hot." Her voice trailed off in another moan as the
blanket scraped over her now engorged nipples.
Looking down she could see that they were slightly
swollen and red with need. Without thinking she trailed
one hand up until she could graze the pad of her finger
over the sensitive nub. The feeling that shot up her chest
was amazing and her panting grew harsher as she forgot
why the sensation was unwanted. Dimly she could hear
a crash and a shrill curse on the other end of the line,
followed by muffled voices and quickly moving
footsteps. It wasn't until she heard the slam of a car
door that Ananda jerked her hand away from her chest
and refocused on the man on the other end of the phone.

"Ananda, listen to me carefully," Jared spoke
quietly yet intensely. Ananda could hear the sound of an
engine being started up and the squealing of tires. "Do
not go near any of the windows or door. Stay in the bed,
and try to stay as quiet as you can."

Nodding and trying not to be alarmed, Ananda once
again trailed a hand to her chest, kneading one breast
with a groan before turning to do the same to the other.
The fact that she could hear Jared cursing softly over
the phone seemed to rile her up even more.

"Are you touching yourself Ananda?" Jared growled, his voice as deep as thunder. It sent a tingle down Ananda's spine and she wished that the man was the one touching her. "Are you feeling your greedy little body? Is your skin hot baby? You want me to be the one touching you don't you?"

"Yes," she hissed, fingers skirting down her flat stomach until they slowly crawled through the dark hair that framed her hidden warmth. "Touching myself and I don't know why. Why is my body so hot? Why do I feel like I'll die without you touching me?" Ananda's fingers reached down further until she found herself drenched with slick and almost unbearably sensitive to the touch. Despite Jared's admonishment to stay as quiet as possible, Ananda couldn't help the needy grunts and groans that escaped as she slipped two fingers into her pulsing channel. She was so slick that there was no discomfort, only a feeling of 'yes.'

"Ananda," Jared growled. She had forgotten that she still had him on the phone, so caught up in the demands of her body.

Whining, Ananda tried to focus. "Tell me. Why do I feel this way? Please…"

Chapter Two

The sound of screeching tires sounded almost too loud to be coming from the phone and Ananda jerked when she heard the door to the room being flung open until it crashed against the wall. Seeing Jared standing in the doorway, eyes wild and chest heaving was the missing piece, and Ananda found herself flung head-first into a powerful orgasm. When she came back she was once again gathered in Jared's strong arms as the man slowly caressed her damp cheek.

"You're in, well I guess the easiest way to explain is to say you're in heat. It's something we all go through in our twenty-first year. Our bodies are going through the last maturation stage which is full sexual maturity." Jared's voice wavered slightly as Ananda began to slowly writhe, succumbing to the throes of passion once again. She turned watery eyes upward to gaze at the man and swallowed as his nostrils flared, eyes dilated until there was only a small ring of blue left.

"Jared," she whined, frantically reaching to pull the man down to her lips. Though the heat had quieted slightly with his soft touch against her cheek it just wasn't enough and she desperately needed to feel his heated body against her own. She could feel his body hardening underneath her back and she wondered why he didn't just take what they both wanted.

"Because I want you to be sure," Jared answered, fingers carding through her hair as he sent calming thoughts through their already forming bond. He shifted their bodies around until he was reclining slightly with Ananda resting between his outstretched legs. He slowly and carefully began massaging her shoulders and arms, transferring his feelings of calm to his fingertips and willing her heat to recede. Though her scent was incredibly enticing, he was being truthful when he said he wanted her to be sure before things went further between them. He wouldn't be like Jenny, he wouldn't treat Ananda as disposable. Nor could he place the burden on her of being matched with him for a lifetime before she truly got the chance to live and experience life.

As if sensing Jared's inner musings, Ananda curled her hand into his squeezing in what she hoped was understood reassurance. "I get it Jared. I really do. I'm being ruled by my emotions, pulled along by my maturing libido, blah blah blah." She tried to take a calming breath and get her thoughts in order. "The thing is…you smell really good to me, and you feel really good to me. Now, I might not completely know what that means, but the fact that in all of the people I've ever slept with, not once has it all hit me like that at once."

A low humming growl filled the air as Jared's chest rumbled soothingly against Ananda's back relaxing her even further.

"You smell good to me too," Jared whispered, nose sliding up the sensitive skin behind her ear as he took in more of her scent in deep controlled breaths. "But you should know everything about us before you do something and later regret it."

"But I want you so bad," Ananda whined, turning swiftly to face his lips, meeting in a kiss that she swore she could feel deep in her core. Deep down Ananda knew this man. She knew Jared; his story, his life, his very essence called to her in a way that could never be matched by another human being. His protests and inclination to create space between them was completely unacceptable and she knew that even while he pulled away, it wasn't what he truly wanted.

Jared was trying so hard to do the noble thing, turn Ananda away until she was lucid enough to really think about the possible ramifications of their actions. Already a bond was building between them that would be a pain to sever, but if they didn't stop now, if they allowed it to continue and strengthen it would be damn near impossible to reverse without serious complications to one or both of them. He didn't want to; God knows he didn't. Everything in him was screaming to cement their connection, to bury himself so far in her that even those with no abilities would somehow be able to sense that they belonged to one another. It was this part of himself that deepened their kiss, making him shift until he was prone against the bed, Ananda's quickly reheating body straddling his hips and pushing her molten core against his hardened shaft. It took everything within him to hold her still when all he really wanted to do was unzip his jeans and once again lose himself in her silky depths.

"Trust me when I say," he panted, pulling away from her sinfully reddened lips. "I want to destroy you with my cock." Unable to help himself, he dove in again, easily prodding her lips apart in order to taste her warmth. "I want to carve a spot so deep inside you that no one but me could ever fill it." The sound of her heated whimper made his rigid prick pulse with want, and almost without thinking he deftly unzipped his pants, pulling himself out and shuddering at his sensitivity.

"Do it Jared, please. I need you and I know you need me." Ananda shifted lower until she could feel the head of Jared's heated shaft lined up against her folds. If not for the man's hesitation she would have plunged herself downward taking all of him into her core. But she could feel the need for him to choose her as if her body would not be satisfied unless a clear decision was made either way. "I need a mate, Jared, my other half. I've been looking for him for so long and now I know…" she trailed off, gasping as one of his hands dug into the meat of her rear.

Jared could feel himself slipping. "You know what?" he hissed, taking Ananda's bottom lip between his teeth and pulling back with a groan. "Tell me what you know. Tell me what you need."

He could feel it; they were poised on a precipice, waiting for that one word…

Opening her eyes, Ananda smiled softly before leaning to rest her lips against his.

"You."

As if hit by a bolt of lightning, Jared's body tightened before plunging into the warm abyss of the woman above. The sound of Ananda's wail of triumph spurred a symphony of growls from Jared as his body sought to fulfill his partner's needs. The air was saturated with the scent of honey and citrus as their pheromones co-mingled and merged, signifying the meshing of souls. The sound of skin meeting skin was deafening as their bodies surged against one another, racing steadily towards the finish line of their climax. Open mouths met as uneven breaths were shared back and forth, neither party able to turn it into a true kiss. With a final snap of his hips, Jared was flung into an orgasm so powerful he swore he'd gone blind. The feeling of warmth surging through her lower body made Ananda clench as her body was hurled over the precipice and into ecstasy while once again everything went black.

Chapter Three

Kerri slowly entered the apartment, dropping her keys onto the table by the door just like she had done countless times before. She knew that it would be empty, Ananda having been taken somewhere else by the stranger who had been tailing them for weeks. It was good that he had come just in time to spirit her friend away, promising to keep the other girl safe from everyone, including herself. It had been an issue that Kerri didn't know quite know how to handle, keeping Ananda safe from the organization that wanted to eradicate people like her, the very same organization that Kerri's father owned. The young woman had known as soon as she met Ananda that she needed to find a way to keep her off of her father's radar, and had been secretly making a plan for months until she realized another person had taken interest in the auburn-haired beauty.

"Hello cousin."

Sighing with annoyance, Kerri turned to the living room to see Jenny sitting casually on the couch as if it were something she did every day. While she could see her cousin smiling, the sentiment never quite reached her eyes, which stayed as cold and blank as one would expect from a killer.

"What are you doing here Jenny? I told my father I wanted nothing to do with his mindless quest for world domination or whatever." Disinterested, Kerri walked into the kitchen noting that the other woman followed her without prompting. She snorted as she pictured a fluffy little Pomeranian with sharp teeth which perfectly fit what she thought of her cousin. Truthfully, Kerri cared little for any of the members of her so-called family. Other than the blood pumping through her veins she had little in common with them and actively tried to distance herself in every way possible. If not for her gift of shielding her thoughts and the thoughts of others, she could pretend that she had come from another family and had simply been adopted at birth. In her mind that would have been preferable to being born into what she saw as a fucked up underground system consisting of her family and those that they routinely tried to either convince to work for them or eradicated.

"Oh I'm not here for you my little basket case," Jenny smirked as she lifted an apple from the table. She inspected the fruit carefully before taking a bite and chewing thoughtfully. "No, I'm here to see your roommate. You know, the one you said was just another normal human, boring and clueless." Turning wicked blue eyes to survey the woman in front of her, Jenny took another bite of the apple before a dangerous glint appeared in her eye. "Turns out she may not be as clueless or boring as you'd originally reported."

Kerri shrugged, trying to appear nonchalant and uncaring about the subject. "I don't know nor do I care what you're talking about. My roommate, as you can see, isn't here. You probably scared her off by, oh I don't know, breaking into our apartment!" The last part was said with barely disguised anger. Kerri had tried so hard to protect Ananda from being discovered and yet she had the worst feeling that her protectiveness may have been what led her family right to her. Trying her damndest to stay calm, Kerri finished her glass of water and carefully placed the cup in the sink before turning once again to face her cousin.

"Look, I told my father I wanted no part in his mindless quest to subdue and coerce innocent people into going along with his machinations. He agreed to leave me alone indefinitely, so why the fuck did I come home to find you in my house, looking for my roommate and disrupting my goddamn life?"

"I interrupted your life?" Jenny's eyes narrowed as she took a step closer to the seething red head. "Wake up princess. This isn't a life, it's a lie. You lie to yourself every day that you wake up and pretend to be just a normal human girl. You're not. Get over it and get with the fucking program." Jenny removed a dagger from her pocket and slammed it on the kitchen counter. Kerri could see it was the ceremonial dagger her father had given to her when she reached 13, the age all children were tested to see if they were gifted. She had abandoned it when she moved out of the family home and excommunicated herself from the others. "You knew that your roommate was one of them; a danger to everyone around her and yet you allowed her to go around undetected. You were willing to risk the lives of others in order to feed some bullshit rebellion against your family."

"I did no such thing!" Kerri screeched, hands balling into fists as her emotions got the best of her.

"Think about how many people could have been hurt or killed if that thing had lost control!"

"Ananda isn't like that!"

"She's a killer!"

"She's my friend!" Kerri screamed, hands coming up and burying themselves in the collar of Jenny's shirt. "She would never hurt anyone and I know it. You all are just too stupid and ruled by fear to stop and think about all of the lives you've ruined with this pointless crusade!" Gathering her strength, Kerri lashed out pushing her cousin away from her. She looked away from the other woman as hot tears threatened to fall from her burning eyes. "Get out."

Jenny gathered herself from the floor, eyes still locked on the petite redhead. "Your feelings cloud your judgment cousin. One day Ananda will lose control, and when she does it will be forever etched on your conscience. I hope you're ready to deal with that."

Turning back to her cousin, Kerri's eyes were blank as she closed off her mind. "Leave my house and never return. I want nothing to do with any of you. And you can tell the man I used to call father, the next time he sends one of you to follow me or do harm to Ananda in any way, I'll return you myself, in a body bag. Have I made myself clear?"

"…Crystal," Jenny answered, turning on her heel and heading towards the door.

Kerri stood in the kitchen, long after the door had been closed, mind rolling with half-formed thoughts. It took her many hours to find sleep that night.

Chapter Four

The next morning, Ananda woke up again with a heavy arm draped around her waist, but this time her body was back to a normal temperature. She did ache slightly, but smiled as the images from last night played again in her mind. Frantic sex had gradually given way to slow and sensual love making as Jared took his time and showed her all of the things she had been missing from her previous partners. Slowly untangling her limbs from the still snoozing man's, she walked into the bathroom and started a warm bath that would help soothe her aching muscles. Ananda gazed at her image in the mirror, hand coming up to touch the dark bruise at the base of her neck that was evidence from the past evening's events. It made her preen inside to carry the mark from Jared and she wanted to show it off to the world to that she had been claimed by him. Her golden eyes almost seemed to glow with happiness. She stepped into the steaming water, groaning at the feeling of warmth and adding a few drops of lavender oil to the bath water. The scent went a long way towards helping relax her and she leaned her head back relaxing further into the tub.

Ananda wasn't sure how long she sat there letting the warmth from the water creep into her weary muscles but she soon became aware of noises coming from the room. Thinking that Jared had finally woken up, she called out to him.

"Hey, come join me in the bath! I found some lavender oil that is really…" Her sentence was cut off as a dark figure hurled itself into the bathroom covering her mouth with its hand and trapping her startled scream. Ananda struggled, limbs flailing and water pouring out of the tub as the figure began calling her name frantically.

"Ananda!"

Ananda shot up out of bed, breath coming in harsh pants as she struggled to make sense of what was happening. Quickly she became aware of her surroundings and found herself sitting in bed, Jared holding her shoulders with panic clear on his face. "What happened?" Ananda asked. It didn't make any sense. Wasn't she in the bath?

"You started yelling in your sleep like someone was trying to kill you. What happened? What did you see?" Jared questioned frantically confusing the woman even more.

"What do you mean what did I see? Aren't I supposed to be able to influence people?" Ananda was confused and growing more alarmed as Jared stood up and began to quickly circle the room packing up what little supplies they had brought with them. He collected their food from the floor, throwing Ananda her clothes and motioning for her to quickly get dressed.

"Not everyone has the same gift. We're all born with the ability to read other's minds and somewhat sense emotions, but once we turn of age sometimes we gain a new gift and that could be anything from being able to influence others to starting fires with our minds.

It's why people hunt us down to either capture us or kill us." Finally dressed, Jared grabbed his bag before hustling Ananda out of the room and back into the car. His eyes darted back and forth taking everything in as they pulled out of the parking lot and back on the road. Ananda was quiet as she took in everything that she had learned so far. Finding out that she might somehow have gained the ability to see the future was almost too fantastical to believe.

"So I can see the future. God, how much more of a freak could I possibly be!" Ananda was incensed. She felt herself relax when Jared's hand reached over and covered her own where she had slowly been tightly squeezing her thigh.

"Ananda, no matter what anyone says, you are not a freak. There's nothing wrong with either of us and don't let anyone tell you otherwise." The man's conviction went far to reassure Ananda that although she might be going through some changes, deep down inside she hadn't really changed. She was still her.

"So what happened? Why was someone in my apartment and why are we still running?" Now that Ananda calmed down, she was back to focusing on their first meeting and why Jared was even in the alley in the first place. "And what happened with Kerri?"

Taking his time to gather his thoughts, Jared tightened his hands on the steering wheel, eyes staring straight ahead. "There are people who know what we can do and they seek to use us for a lot of different reasons. And others think we are dangerous and want to eradicate us from the Earth."

Ananda was a bit startled by the information. "Wait, why do some people think we're dangerous?" The question made Jared breathe deeply as he struggled with reawakened guilt from the past.

"There have been issues with those of us who struggle with the gift. Hearing voices isn't considered…normal I guess, and some of us can't handle it and lose touch with reality." Jared took a deep breath before deciding to be completely honest with the woman he wanted to be with. He knew that starting their relationship based on lies would only create more problems as time went on. "When I was in high school, there was a kid that everyone bullied. I knew he had the gift because I could hear his thoughts, dark thoughts about silencing the voices and I wanted…" Jared's breath shuttered as he tried hard not to let his feelings of his past overwhelm him. Ananda couldn't take her eyes off of Jared, a feeling of dismay filling her mind. She could feel the distress flowing off of the man in waves. Her comfort gave Jared the strength to continue.

"I wanted to tell him he wasn't alone, but I was terrified. I had only recently gotten control of my own ability and my parents weren't talking about sending me away for treatment anymore and I thought that if I said something, they would think I had a relapse. So I stayed quiet; I didn't talk to the kid any more than necessary and I didn't tell anyone what he was thinking."

Ananda could feel herself horribly fascinated. It was as if she could picture what happened in her mind's eye. Somehow she saw the boy from Jared's story enter into a cafeteria, intent on silencing the voices that repeatedly tormented him. Looking around she saw jocks laughing and pointing, their words cruel and biting. She saw a table of girls throwing looks at the young man, disgust clearly evident on their young faces. And yet through it all, she could see one lone figure, a girl with a cascade of dark hair, high cheek bones and eyes of indescribable color and somehow she knew, this girl was Jared's sister. Unbelievably, for a moment the two girls' eyes connected and Ananda knew that she was being seen as surely as she knew what would happen next.

"Take care of him," the other girl whispered as chaos erupted in the cafeteria and a jolt unlike one Ananda had ever experienced pushed her consciousness back into the present where Jared was worriedly staring at her. She was unsurprised to find tears in her eyes as a sob worked its way from her throat.

"I saw her Jared," Ananda whispered, throat raspy with emotion. "I saw Sophie."

Though he had pledged to himself to keep Ananda safe, he was unprepared for the effect her scent would have on him. He found himself hardening fast, and even though they were surrounded by the stench of trash and waste, the desire to bend her over and have her right then and there was damn near overwhelming. Only the thought of being caught by whoever had been hunting him kept him from doing something incredibly stupid in the alley. No, he will save it for later.

In retrospect, being contained in a small space with the object of your desire spilling fresh pheromones everywhere probably wasn't the best idea he had ever had. If he had been a better man, he would have gotten two separate rooms and retreated to take care of his sexual frustration alone. He may have been able to control himself if not for the innocent thought that drifted his way.

"Why do you smell so good?"

The realization that Ananda could smell him as much as he could smell her broke whatever control Jared thought he had and before he could regain his senses he found himself balls deep, buried in a warmth that threatened to break the tenuous hold he had on his feelings. Every thrust felt like a cleansing and every gasp and moan like the words of an angel. Afterwards as he lay beside her sleeping body, Jared's eyes took in everything about her from the point of her nose to the ample swelling of her bosom. Somehow in the midst of so much chaos and pain, he had managed to find the woman who would complete him. He didn't know how he knew, but he just knew. And now that he had her wrapped safely in his arms, he dared anyone to try to come and rip them apart.

He knew that this battle wasn't over; it hadn't even truly begun. For some reason there were people out there hunting people like him and Ananda, and Jared would not rest until he could be sure that the woman asleep in his arms would be safe.

To be continued in Book 4

Book Four - Revealed

Chapter One

JARED WAS quiet for the next few hours as they continued their drive. He hadn't responded when Ananda explained that she had seen his sister and the message she had given her. The idea that not only had Sophie known about her brother's gift but somehow also had the gift herself was alarming and Ananda just knew that asking questions now would be a bad move. So rather than talk and risk upsetting the man further, Ananda decided to catch up on as much sleep as possible. She was still unsure of their destination and secretly she was terrified that the dark figure from her vision would find them before they reached whatever destination they were heading to.

"I'm sorry." The sound of Jared's voice was almost overly loud in the quiet of the car. Ananda opened her eyes but refused to turn around. Somehow she knew that whatever the man needed to say, it would be much easier for him to get it out if she weren't looking at him. "I'm not angry with you…it's just…" Jared paused, as if to gather courage. "The whole time we were growing up, Sophie never ever told me she had a gift. Not even when I started hearing voices and told her. I always thought that if I had done more, I could have saved her that day. If only I had told someone about Kevin instead of hiding away like a coward. Or if I had stayed in the cafeteria that day…"

"Then you would have died along with everyone else and you wouldn't have been here, now, alive and able to keep me from being caught or killed by whoever is after me!" Ananda couldn't help but turn to look at the man. The sound of his grief was almost more than she could bear. "I didn't know your sister, but I'm sure she would never have wanted you to be there that day. She was your big sister and for some reason… for some reason that I just can't explain, I know she knew what was going to happen."

If not for his iron grip on the steering wheel, Jared might have jerked out of his seat with shock. "What?" He couldn't wrap his head around the thought. Even if Sophie had had the gift, she wasn't old enough for extra abilities to have manifested. "She wasn't old enough to have that ability. Abilities like that don't manifest until after maturation."

"I know... I know you said that but… I don't know how to explain it Jared." She put her hand softly on Jared's shoulder, willing him to understand what she saw and felt. Suddenly a tingling sensation manifested almost like an itch behind her ear. The feeling traveled down her arm and into the tips of her fingers as they rested against Jared's warm skin until she was sure that the man had to be feeling something. It was odd how surely Ananda felt about Jared when they had only met one another seventy-two hours ago. She spared a thought for Kerri and wondered what her dearest friend was doing in her absence. "Do you think I could call Kerri, or my parents? I mean, would it be safe to call them? They aren't in any danger, right?"

Jared thought carefully before he decided what to say. "Ananda, how much do you know about your roommate Kerri?" he questioned, glancing over at the girl before reaffixing his focus back to the desolate road in front of him. Thankfully they had made good time getting out of the city and were close enough to their first stop in Rochester that he felt he could relax just a little. Jared hadn't been looking forward to cluing Ananda in to who her friend really was, or the family that she left behind, but he knew that in order to keep the woman he had come to care for safe, he needed to be completely honest and if that meant divulging some uncomfortable truths then so be it.

On her end, Ananda was struck dumb by the question. "What do you mean? I know she comes from a big family and has, I think, two or three brothers and sisters. Her dad was a real piece of work though and he treated them all terribly." She couldn't figure out why Jared was so intent on information about Kerri.

"Did any of them ever visit you guys at school? Did you ever meet her family even once?" Jared glanced over quickly again noting the woman's perplexed expression. "Think carefully, Ananda. This is important. Did you ever meet any of Kerri's family?"

"No I..." Ananda tried to think back over the past three years of her and Kerri's friendship. She remembered meeting Kerri randomly at one of the freshman activities and being in awe at first of the other girl's exuberant personality and then later relieved at the quietness of her mind. Despite the fact that they had shared almost three full years together, first as friends and then as roommates, not once did she ever meet the other girl's family. In fact, regardless of all the times she brought Kerri back to meet her family, there was never a reciprocated offer. It was as if Kerri's family life was completely separate from her life at school with Ananda. The realization made something heavy settle into her gut and she wondered how she could've been so blind as to not be suspicious that in all the time she'd known Kerri, not once had she thought to question it. It made her heart beat faster at the thought of Kerri being somehow involved with the people chasing them. What if it had been Kerri who let the person into their apartment?

"She didn't."

Ananda was startled by Jared's voice breaking her inner dialogue of betrayal and confusion. Slowly she looked up until their eyes met, hers shining with the moisture of unshed tears in the face of her best friend's possible duplicity.

"She didn't betray you, Ananda. This I know for a fact," Jared could still feel the woman's simmering feelings of sadness and hurt.

"How do you know?" Ananda looked down as her hands tightened into fists. How could she have been so stupid? A large strong hand came over and settled on top of hers; a thumb rubbing the back of one hand until she forced them to relax. Taking a deep breath, Ananda tangled her fingers with Jared's, trying not to blush at her boldness but feeling the need to be close and seek comfort.

"Because she told me, or she thought it at me rather," Jared stumbled over his wording trying his best to comfort Ananda and yet make her see what they were up against. "In all the time you have known her, not once have you been able to get a read on her thoughts, just vague emotions right?"

"Yeah."

"And she never took you to meet her family or invited them over when you were around?"

"Yeah… no, never. She made it seem like there had been a falling out or something. Like maybe she was estranged from them I think, something about her not living up to her father's expectations. She was always really angry about it and yet totally vague. Though…honestly, I think it might have been because of a high school boyfriend… her dad didn't approve and kept them apart…" Ananda trailed off unsure as Jared nodded to himself. He'd always wondered how the organization that hunted people like them continued to operate, targeting younger and younger subjects.

"Look, remember the organization I talked about that is hunting people like us? Well, it's her family or rather they were her family if what you said is true about her being estranged. I was kind of surprised to see you two so close given who or what she is, but it definitely makes sense. Her father probably hunted that boyfriend of hers and that's what the catalyst of the estrangement was. Perhaps we can use your relationship…"

"No!" Ananda jerked her hands back away from Jared's and turned away. Everything in her life had been so perfect until this gift of hers fucked it all up.

"Ana, I'm not saying that we should take advantage of Kerri or anything, but it's clear that she loves you like a sister and I'm sure she doesn't want us getting caught or you getting hurt. She probably blames herself right now for not telling you who she really was."

"I don't," Ananda swallowed hard against the lump in her throat, desperately trying to hold back the tears that threatened to fall as she watched the trees go passing by. She could hear the sound of Jared shifting in his seat, but was still caught by surprise when his arm lay softly across her shoulder.

"Then we won't, okay?" Breathing deeply, Jared decided to just go with what he was feeling instead of trying to fight or hide it. "I want to protect you using any means possible and I know your friend Kerri wants to do the same. For now we'll just worry about getting as far away as possible before deciding our next move. I have a few contacts in Toronto who can help us set up new identities and new lives which should hopefully keep us off the radar for a good long while."

"But, what will I tell my parents? How will I finish school?" Ananda sat up, eyes red-rimmed from her tears as she thought about all the hard work she had done over the past three years. Truthfully, she had been undecided on her major and had only recently decided to stick with psychology, but the thought of abandoning her life… the life she had had for twenty-one years, was enough to send her into a panic. Ananda clenched her hands into fists. 'Fuck, I'm not going to cry again!' She had just stopped her tears and already they were threatening to overwhelm her again. Her heart started to once again beat unsteadily and what little food she had eaten at the last rest stop was threatening to make a reappearance in a hurry. She already lost her parents once when her gifts had manifested the first time. She didn't want to lose them again, or her brother Ryan. And then what about Kerri and the other friends she had made at the university? True, she hadn't really bothered to keep in touch with those friends as much, and it had been months since she had been in touch with Ryan or her parents. Oh God, what if everything had been going this way for a reason. Maybe her parents would be happier with her gone?

Suddenly, Ananda's chest went tight and she gasped, unable to slow her breathing. She ground her teeth together to brace herself for the panic attack she knew was bearing down on her with startling quickness. Distantly Ananda could hear Jared's voice calling out to her, his hand cupping her cheek. Her body began to shake uncontrollably and it felt like the world suddenly tilted on its axis as Jared roughly jerked the wheel, turning into a motel parking lot. Dimly Ananda was aware of the passenger side door being opened and her body being lifted out, Jared carrying her bridal-style into a dimly lit room and locking the latch behind him. She could only barely breathe as her body refused to cease its shaking. Her head was pounding as Ananda curled into a fetal position wishing that someone would just put her out of her misery.

Instead she got Jared's voice, gruff and yet soft, whispering sweet things into her ear that she had no hope of understanding while she was in her panicked state. She could feel a hand running gingerly through her hair, stopping to massage at her temples and sending calming feelings in their wake. The panic began to fade, leaving the hurt behind as Ananda became more aware of her surroundings. She could feel Jared curled up behind her, his warmth and scent doing wonders at calming her down.

"It's okay my love," Jared whispered, voice soft and soothing to Ananda's shot nerves. "We'll be okay. Just relax and sleep. I'll be here for you when you wake and we'll figure out together what to do. Just trust me and let go." For a moment Ananda considered fighting back and raging, but the warmth and concern in the man's voice lessened the terrible pressure in her aching chest and soon enough sleep claimed her for its own.

Jared watched over Ananda while she slept. Her panic attack brought on by realizing that everything she had ever known was gone had riled Jared more than he let on. Truthfully, she wasn't the only one who would have to let go of the life she had once known. He'd never be able to visit his parents and grieve together or visit Sofie's grave without worrying that someone might spot him. His parents would have to deal with the pain of essentially losing both of their children, which wasn't something he had ever let himself think about even after he'd become aware of the organization that was hunting him. Somewhere in the back of his mind he had hoped that it was all just a big misunderstanding, but now he realized that his desire to have life remain the same may be what was hindering him from moving on. Looking down at Ananda's sleep tossed hair and forlorn expression even in sleep made something powerful bloom in his chest. He would do anything for this woman, and if that meant abandoning the life he'd known then so be it. He knew that with Ananda by his side, he could build a better future and work towards one day not having to look over his shoulder or hide his abilities. He could learn to love himself and maybe even find a happiness greater than what he had ever known.

Shifting, Jared extended his mind out to see if anyone had been tailing them. All he heard were some rather inappropriate conversations and prayers and so he allowed himself to relax slightly. He knew he wouldn't be able to fully let himself unwind until they were across the border and safely ensconced in his friend Bill's safe house. For now he would give himself a moment's reprieve to enjoy the closeness he shared with Ananda.

Chapter Two

The feeling of shifting and long heavy sighs woke Jared up a few hours later and he tightened the arm that was draped around Ananda's waist. "Again?" he intoned sleepily, nose buried behind Ananda's ear and taking in the honey sweetness that was starting to waft from her. Truly he didn't mind being woken up by her need for sex; if anything he hoped that it would become a regular sort of thing in their lives. Reaching up, Jared turned Ananda's head slightly, enough to where he could capture her already bite-reddened lips with his own. The kiss started out innocent enough until Ananda's groan sent over pleasant vibrations that turned the kiss into something deeper and more passionate. Soon enough, Jared found himself kneeling above Ananda, one arm propping him up while the other tried its damndest to rid them of their clothing. Ananda parted her lips in order to allow Jared's tongue to stroke over her own as her legs fell further apart. Her hands came up, one clasping Jared's upper arm in a tight grip while the other hand ran slight fingernails over the man's back.

Jared broke away gasping for breath and shuddering hard at the sensation of Ananda's nails against his skin. Leaning down, he shifted slightly in order to suck stinging kisses into the skin of Ananda's neck.

"Jared," Ananda moaned, hips shifting and raising. Upon contact with Jared's tightened body, she let out a louder groan grinding against him in tight circles. Jared answered with a bite to Ananda's collarbone as he fought to keep himself from thrusting back and ending things too prematurely.

Ananda tried again to draw his attention to the place she really needed it. "Jared, come on. Please touch me. God at least get my pants off and your pants off. I'd really like to be naked so I can come…and then make you come…repeatedly." Jared made a hungry noise in the back of his throat before rocking back to perch on his heels. He unbuttoned Ananda's jeans and moved slowly back, peeling them off as he went. Slowly Ananda's overheated skin was revealed to the cooler heat of the room. She shivered slightly as goose bumps rose on her sensitive skin. He trailed his lips down the woman's body, stopping occasionally to linger over a spot that made Ananda's back arch with pleasure. Soon his open-mouthed and wet kisses slid to the skin of her inner thigh and breathing deeply the smell of her arousal, cloying and honey sweet. Jared's gaze was so hot that Ananda did not even have time to be self-conscious of her half naked state. She sat up slightly, crossing both arms at her chest in order to pull her shirt and bra off enjoying the hitch in Jared's breathing as he stared at her newly uncovered body.

Enjoying the gaze on her and yet wanting more, Ananda pawed weakly at Jared's clothes before demanding, "Clothes off." She managed to unbutton his jeans before his brain rebooted and he helped her rid him of the offending jeans and shirt. Ananda got a very brief eyeful of Jared's naked body: his toned flat stomach that lead to thickly muscled thighs and the long hard cock between them that stood almost begging for Ananda's attention. It was as if Ananda was seeing Jared for the first time. True that she had already had him inside of her, but from this angle she truly got an idea of how big the man was and her mouth watered at the sight of him. She pushed the man until he was on his side before sliding down to get a better view of the thickness she longed to have inside of her. Her hand curled around Jared's impressive length and she breathed in deep the scent of citrus and musk that she had come to associate as 'Jared'. She could see that his length was already slick at the tip, his head flushed a dark red color. Without waiting to see what the man would do, Ananda leaned further down to lap at the warm head, humming as his taste burst out across her taste buds.

Jared fought hard not to let his hips thrust with the first feeling of Ananda's tongue against his swollen prick. One of his hands reached down to comb through her hair, not pushing but just holding on and enjoying the woman's explorations. Looking down Jared could see a hint of a smile on Ananda's lips before she dipped down and took him in a bit further, her hands covering what little she couldn't fit into her mouth. Her cheeks hollowed as she expertly provided suction with every withdrawal. It wasn't long before he was close to the edge, cock being expertly worked and stimulated with every thrust of Ananda's sinful mouth and the noises of enjoyment she couldn't seem to contain. Shifting slightly to grip Ananda under the arms, Jared pulled her back up the bed and once again cuddled in close, propping himself up on an elbow. He looked down at the woman who had changed him and leaned in to kiss her again, stroking one large hand along her heated cheeks.

Ananda could still taste the slick from Jared's hard cock and it made her feel warm and alive. She felt no shame in her enjoyment as she sought to give her body what it craved.

"I want you to fuck me, Jared."

The man's hips jerked, clearly liking the idea of once again being buried in her tight sheath. "That's kind of intense baby. Remember you were in a lot of pain afterwards last time." Jared's fingers slid down her side pulling her leg up until it rested across his hips. This gave him access to the source of her biggest pleasure and Jared wanted to make sure he gave Ananda everything before taking his own enjoyment. Reaching back down, Jared enjoyed hearing a hitch in the woman's breathing as one finger slid along her slick folds.

"I wasn't in pain Jared, I was just a bit sore," Ananda answered breathily as her hips began to shift in time with the man's finger. "You are the biggest I've ever had…so far anyway." The last part of her sentence was accompanied by a smirk that made the man want to growl. Instead he slid two fingers inside of Ananda's heated core with no warning, causing the woman to arch back with a pleasured yell.

"The biggest you've had so far, eh? You planning on finding someone else to fill you up like I do baby?" Jared curled his fingers slightly knowing exactly where to press to see Ananda shiver with spiking arousal.

"Well, first you should definitely put your dick in me," Ananda chimed breathlessly trying to shift in order to get the man's fingers to press deeper into her. To her chagrin, Jared sat up splaying one arm effortlessly over the woman's hips in order to keep her from moving. Ananda never thought her fantasies included being pinned down and ravished to within an inch of her life, but obviously she was wrong.

"Fuck, please fuck me Jared!" Ananda was just trying to rile Jared up with her teasing. There would never be anyone else who could fill her up and make her want like Jared. Just the thought of the man driving his hardened cock into her was enough to make Ananda drip steadily with arousal. Jared swallowed deeply and Ananda was so distracted that she almost missed Jared's next words.

"I know, God I want you too baby. I just don't want to rush this. I want us to take our time and really explore…" Ananda's hand came up and harshly slapped itself across the man's mouth effectively cutting him off.

"I know you want to make every moment we have together special Jar, and I promise next time we can go as fast or as slow as you want. You can tie me up and play with me for hours or use my mouth to get off. Whatever you want okay baby? But next time. Right now I need you to get inside me as quickly as possible until I can't even remember my own name—,"

"A gag would be pretty useful for you as well," Jared interrupted, his thumb moving to circle around Ananda's sensitive clitoris. The feeling has her shuddering deep and Jared groaned at feeling her silky channel contract around his finger.

"That's fine, whatever you want Jared just—," Ananda started to babble until Jared abruptly slid his fingers from her quivering sheath. The feeling of being so fucking empty made Ananda keen with want and she swore she could feel her aching hole pulsing with the need to be stretched and filled by Jared once again.

The man pushed Ananda slightly until she was on her back, legs spread as far as they could go before he settled in between, cock just resting outside her pulsating channel. Jared's dick nudged at the inside of her thigh and what was left of Ananda's brain went completely offline. She whined as her fingertips dug into the skin of Jared's upper arms, begging him without words to end her torture. The man leaned down until his mouth was right next to her ear. "Like this?" He murmured using one hand to prop him up and the other the guide the head of his cock until it rested just at Ananda's greedy, wanting entrance.

"Yeah," she said, mind gone elsewhere as her body did nothing but respond to its own needs.

"Lift up. No, lift your hips. Yeah there you go baby."

Ananda obligingly lifted her hips and Jared shoved a pillow under her lower back before turning all of his attention back to her. "Stop me if it hurts okay? I know you want it, but I'm big and I don't ever want to hurt you."

Ananda opened her eyes and smiled. Her hand slid along Jared's skin until it rested on his stubbly cheeks. "Your dick is big yeah, but it isn't like a monster or any—" She forgot to finish her sentence when Jared began pressing forward. Her entrance offered up a small token of resistance before surrendering gracefully and soon Ananda realized that Jared's cock was firmly nestled within her. For just a second the feeling was almost too much, too alien and then when Ananda thought the feeling would consume her alive, she opened her eyes and looked up. When her and Jared's eyes met, it was as if the room they were in fell away and all that was left was the pleasure between them. Her limbs almost felt as if they were getting looser and Ananda marveled at how new and wondrous sex felt with Jared.

The man shifted and a slow spark slithered up Ananda's spine. Jared leaned down for another toe-curling kiss and Ananda closed her eyes again to lose herself in the feeling of closeness and safety that was making love to Jared. She ran her fingers through the man's soft thick mane and down his neck, the desire to touch him everywhere making her slightly frantic with its presence. When he started to move, her hands gripped onto his shoulders tightly, causing a groan to flow from his mouth and into her own.

The slow drag of Jared's cock sent sparks along Ananda's spine and she shivered with the feeling. "Jared," she sighed, back arching slightly. The man leaned down to nuzzle the soft skin of her neck, leaving small open-mouthed kisses that made Ananda's breath puff out unsteadily. He kept his rhythm steady and unhurried, basking in the feeling of finally being close to another person without worrying that they would betray him in the morning. The feeling of joy at being buried deeply in Ananda's body threatened to shake tears from Jared's own eyes and his brow furrowed slightly with concentration focusing on keeping his pace steady and not being too much of a sap.

Ananda had no such qualms about her emotions and freely let the tears fall from her eyes and wet the pillow underneath her. Reaching up, she buried her hands in Jared's hair and tugged him up until their mouths met again, wet and uncoordinated. "Jared please…" Ananda arched her hips up with the next thrust making them collide with more force. Somewhere inside of her, a light turned on zapping her nerve endings and pushing her closer and closer to the precipice of her desire. She pushed up against him, trying to make him quicken his pace and moaning loudly between dirty wet kisses.

Despite Ananda's pleas, Jared's pace never quickened and it drove her almost mindless with lust. Soon she was moaning with every thrust and begging loudly for Jared to end his torturous pace. "Just Jared! I need it, need you. Please harder, fuck me harder."

Jared's eyes darkened as his hips sped up, pausing occasionally to push in deep enough that Ananda's gasps turned into whimpers, her fingers going into spasms against the moist skin of Jared's back. Her toes began to curl with each snap of the man's hips and Ananda scrambled to get a better grip on Jared's sweaty shoulders. A few solid thrusts later and Ananda's back arched one last time as her channel tightened around Jared's now pulsing length. For a moment Ananda could swear she'd gone blind, her mind and her body seemingly disconnected with the force of her climax.

When she came back to herself, she could hear Jared moaning her name, his hips thrusting erratically as he chased his own release.

Reaching up to once again tangle her fingers in his hair, Ananda focused on tightening and releasing her still sensitive core as she crooned in his ear. "Fuck me Jared. Come inside me and fill me up. Give me everything," she demanded, nails scraping against the man's scalp and making him shudder. When the man continued, his movements were less fluid with no rhythm. He ground against Ananda until his body tightened and he was flung head first into his climax.

Ananda couldn't help but stare at Jared's face, the face of the man who had come to her when she hadn't even known she needed him and gave her the feeling she had been chasing for so many years. Afterwards, they lay together, legs entwined within tangled sheets and Jared's slowly softening cock still nestled inside of her. The feeling of Jared's warm come sliding out of her is one that Ananda had never thought she would like but knew she would never be able to live without. She knew without a doubt that one day, when they were safe from the people who were hunting them, they would try undeterred by birth control until they made a child: with sharp cheekbones, amber eyes and thick dark hair.

When Jared finally slipped from her body, Ananda stood and entered the bathroom to get some warm towels to clean themselves off. The feeling of now cooling come sliding down her thighs was not one that she was even remotely comfortable with and so she set about changing that. Ananda could hear shuffling in the room and paused suddenly with the feeling that they weren't alone. Suddenly she heard a quiet knock at the door followed by a voice she never thought she'd hear again.

"I know Ananda is here. We all need to talk."

Wrapping a towel hastily around herself, Ananda rushed from the bathroom and came face to face with her brother and…

"Kerri?"

To be continued in Book 5

Book Five - Evasion

Chapter One

JARED FELT anything but relaxed as he sat across from the man who just introduced himself as Ananda's older brother. Typically, he would assume a first meeting with the family of a significant other would include a semi-awkward dinner with the father asking all sorts of probing questions followed by pseudo threats of death by shotgun if a hair on his darling daughter's head was out of place. Instead Jared sat gingerly on the edge of a raggedy bed, clothes having been hastily pulled on in the wake of their new company, with Ananda sobbing in her big brother's arms. A big brother who somehow managed to be comforting to his sister while his eyes promised swift and sudden death to Jared if he found she had come to any harm.

Ananda missed the exchange between her brother and Jared as she pulled back, tears in her eyes and a sob stuck in her throat. Truthfully she had thought she would never see Ryan again and was a bit perplexed by his abrupt re-entry into her life. Her gaze was drawn to how close Ryan and Kerrie were as well as the feeling of raw magnetism that almost radiated between them. Slowly, she backed away until Jared guided her down until she was almost perched across his lap, his arm never leaving the place where it was draped across her waist in a possessive and comforting hold.

"I'm…" Ananda, swallowed hard pushing down the lump in her throat. "It's been months, Ryan. Months! One minute you're telling me about your exploits in the real world; job, house, car, everything. The next you just up and disappear with no phone calls, no emails, nothing!"

"I know Ana and I'm sorry, I really am but," Ryan paused, his gaze sliding over to Kerri as if needing her permission to speak the truth. Ananda could feel her fury rising over her brother and best friend's seemingly unspoken exchange. "We wanted to keep you safe –"

"Keep me safe?!" Ananda exclaimed incredulously. "Were you keeping me safe when you let mom and dad send me to all those shrinks and specialists who made me feel as if I were crazy for hearing voices? Were you keeping me safe when you abandoned me and moved halfway across the country the first chance you got?!" Ananda's voice rang out shrilly as she stood abruptly, fists balled and barely hanging onto what little sanity she had left after the past few days.

"Ananda I know," Ryan started only to be cut off again by his sister's angry voice.

Fighting against Jared's tightening hold around her waist, Ananda could feel fresh hot tears spilling from her eyes and racing down her flushed cheeks. "No you don't Ryan. You don't know shit about anything, especially not how I feel. And you," Ananda turned to the woman she had loved as a sister sitting stock still and unsurprised by Ananda's ire. Her unusual calm almost made Ananda want to rage even harder. "I thought you were my friend and now it seems you'd been lying to me too. How long have you two been plotting and spying on me, huh? Did you have a good laugh at my bumbling efforts to figure out who I was? I should have known something wasn't right when you never invited me to meet your family!"

At the mention of her family, Kerri's countenance changed and her words rang out with a fury greater than Ananda had ever witnessed from the redhead.

"My family is the reason why our lives are so fucked right now!" Kerri used her hands to say the word family in quotations as if the very idea of family was somehow ridiculous. "The reason I've never invited you to meet them is because I washed my hands of them years ago." The slight woman stood abruptly and began pacing as if unable to speak the words while staying still.

"When I was fifteen, my mother, younger sister and I moved to New York. I thought it was strange that my father and brothers didn't come with us, but I figured he had a good reason and didn't dwell on it, instead focusing on school and making friends and trying to be popular." Kerri stopped, turning slowly to look at Ryan, emotion clear in her eyes. "And then I fell in love."

Blinking, Jared looked between the two guests. Without even trying, he could feel the love and affection that practically pulsed off of the two in waves and wondered if he and Ananda were exuding similar feelings.

"I'm so confused right now," Ananda whispered plopping down beside Jared once again. She leaned against him heavily and gladly soaked up the feelings of calm the man was radiating out. She would have had to be a fool to not see the depth of feeling between her brother and Kerri, but it still didn't explain how they knew each other or why they were here now. And how did they even find them?

"I called Bill, whose real name is apparently Ryan and he is also, apparently, your brother," Jared answered.

"Wait," Ananda spoke up. "Didn't you say your friend Bill was in Canada? Wasn't he the guy with safe houses?"

"I am."

"He is."

Covering her face with her hands, Ananda could feel a headache coming on and it threatened to kill what little calm she thought she had regained. She could feel someone move to kneel in front of her and she slowly opened her eyes to see a kaleidoscope of colors staring back at her. Gingerly as if afraid she wouldn't be welcome, Kerri took Ananda's hands in her own.

"I know this is almost too much for you to bear Ana, but please believe me when I say I had no idea Ryan was your brother. I met him when I was fifteen and he was at Columbia. He's part of the reason why my family and I no longer speak." Kerri shifted slightly until she was at eye level with her friend. "When Ryan and I met, he was a lot like you; searching for a reason for his abilities and looking for that special person. We had an instant connection and somehow I just knew that he was it for me."

"I felt it too," Ryan urged running a hand through his thick auburn hair. Jared could see now that he and Ananda looked almost like twins with their thick brown hair and unusual amber eyes. "And trust me when I say I fought it. The thought of having that connection with a kid was devastating and I made damn sure to stay as far away from Kerri as possible."

"Not that I made it easy for him," Kerri laughed as she stood to face Ryan. It was impossible not to see the love in their gazes and Ananda almost felt as if she were encroaching or viewing something not meant for her eyes. "But the same way I knew he was the one for me, I also knew he had the gift and I knew that if my family caught wind of it, of him…" Kerri trailed off, screwing her eyes shut against some unnamed horror that only she knew. Her breathing was coming out in pants and she visibly shook with emotion as Ryan stood and enveloped her in his arms.

"But they found out didn't they? Not just about Ryan, but about someone else," Jared filled in knowingly.

Kerri nodded, unable to hold back the sob as it tore free from her throat. "Thankfully Ryan was graduating. I slipped away one night and tracked him down to warn him about my family and what they would do to him, forcing him to join or die. He got out before they truly got wind of him other than a few half-hearted suspicions. But…" Kerri paused, drawing in a deep breath. "The gift typically manifests itself during the onset of puberty. Because puberty comes at different times for different kids, it's a bit difficult to monitor; however, there are some common signs that my family knows to look out for. Typically there's a sudden onset of doctor visits, specifically hearing specialists and psychologists as well as a sudden withdrawal from normal activities as well as disruptions at school. Once that pattern has been established, each child is monitored, usually by someone their own age who can befriend them enough to report back to the organization."

"But why? Why bother following and spying on us?" Ananda questioned. The whole thing just didn't make sense to her, but Jared knew.

"Kevin."

Kerri was nodding even as Ananda shivered in remembrance. "We were monitoring him before he went off the rails. That's when the family started to really go off the deep end with this crusade of theirs, especially my father. And when my little sister…when she started…" Kerri stopped, breath heaving in and out unsteadily as she lost herself in long buried memories of the past. Ananda couldn't help but feel an overwhelming sense of love for her friend just then and abandoned Jared's side to sweep her friend into a bone crushing hug. The two women sat, holding one another and giving comfort before Kerri felt able to continue.

"When my little sister began to hear the voices, my mother and I tried to hide it as much as possible. I think we both hoped that we could keep her hidden until she learned to control her gift, but my father found out. One day I came home from school and she was just gone." Kerri sighed. "No matter how much my mother and I pleaded with him, my father refused to tell us what happened to her and eventually my mother stopped asking. I just couldn't bear to live there anymore and so I left. I washed my hands of all of them and refused to ever return. I don't even keep in contact with my mother anymore. She is a shell of who she used to be, but she refuses to leave my father no matter how much I beg. I think she's just given up at life."

"So what do we do now?" Ananda asked moving back to Jared's side. Though her brother, Ryan, was with her, she still automatically went to Jared when seeking warmth and comfort, something that did not escape Ryan's attention. His eyes narrowed when Jared's arm circled around his sister, but he seemed to settle when she did. As if the reassurance that Jared cared as much for her as she did for him made the man feel much more comfortable.

"We keep with Jared's plan and head north across the Canadian border. I've got the safe house ready along with new identities and Canadian passports for us. I've gotten a few items to help alter your appearances slightly in order to escape notice for as long as possible. We'll stay here for the night and gather our strength before setting out at dawn. We'll be taking a roundabout way in order to throw off anyone who may be on our trail. Ana," Ryan said abruptly. "I want you to do your best to relax and if you feel anything…out of the ordinary, like someone is following or watching us, I want you to report that straight to me. Right now you are our early warning system and our first line of defense."

Ananda nodded. Her heart was beating slightly faster at the responsibility and she hoped her gift would be enough.

"It will be," Jared replied as if reading her thoughts. He took her hands in his own and leaned down to brush his lips over each knuckle. "You are strong and loyal and brave with more strength than anyone I have ever known. Your gift is powerful and it's already kept us safe once before. Don't doubt yourself, okay?"

Sighing, Ananda tilted her head down in agreement. "I'll do my best," she replied pushing back all seeds of doubt.

After a few more minutes of discussing their escape routes and plans, the two couples split up for the night. Ananda could tell that Ryan and Kerri wouldn't be getting much sleep; with each passing glance, the sexual tension was building to almost unbearable levels before they left. She hoped they remembered to use protection before she flushed at the thought of not following that same advice for herself. It wasn't until Jared spoke again that Ananda realized they were alone.

"What?"

Smiling, Jared shook his head slightly but didn't repeat what he had said. Instead he leaned down to brush his lips against Ananda's own. Ananda would have thought that with everything that had happened and that would probably happen tomorrow, that the kiss would be frantic and a touch desperate in nature. Instead, Jared took his time with the kiss, caressing Ananda's lips with his own in a way that was almost innocent. It was far more tender than either of them had been with one another since the beginning of their liaisons; Ananda found herself falling deeper into her feelings for the man. Her lips relaxed completely as she gave herself over to the feelings of joy and pleasure, a soft moan falling from her lips. Jared picked up on the change and without a word began responding in kind. His lips softened and the kiss seemed to deepen more.

When Jared ended the kiss, it was only to press his lips against the sensitive skin of Ananda's neck. "There's so much I plan to learn and taste about you," he murmured, his tongue peaking out to lick a wet trail across the bare skin. "I want to learn everything about you. It's almost like I'm addicted to your scent and your warm heart. How is it possible to have fallen so deeply for you already?"

Feeling the same way, Ananda slid her hands into Jared's hair, clutching at the thick soft strands and wondering how often she would hear Jared actually discuss his feelings. She figured he probably wouldn't be too keen on constantly talking about them so she reveled in the knowledge while she could. Ananda found herself overwhelmed in an amazing way and almost felt as if she would float away on a cloud of happiness if not for grounding herself with Jared's locks.

"I know we haven't discussed this, but we haven't been using protection," Ananda said as Jared abandoned one side of her neck and attacked the other with equal vigor. Her next words were lost in a sea of feeling as the sensations from her neck caused the lower half of her body to pulse with want. She tried to remind herself of the topic at hand. "It's just, I'm not on birth control and I don't count or track my period so…like, I could be pregnant? Though really it's only been like three days so I doubt I'm pregnant yet, but we could be in for a little surprise in a few weeks if we…"

Jared sat back on his heels, eyes intent as he studied Ananda's face. "So what do you want to do? I mean," rubbing the side of his face, Jared contemplated the merits of being completely honest versus saying what he thought a woman might want to hear.

"I don't know," Ananda sighed in reply. "I mean, I know our life is going to be really crazy soon with running from the organization and relocating to a different country and assuming new identities. Having a baby could make things… no, will make things even more stressful." Ananda frowned as she thought about the difficulties they'd more than likely face over the next few months.

"True, though the last the organization knew, you were totally not pregnant and not even dating anyone. This could give us an advantage by flying under the radar," Jared pointed out. He almost laughed when he saw Ananda's disapproving face.

"That's a horrible reason to have a child, Jared!" Ananda exclaimed, outraged that the man would even suggest that. At Jared's amused expression, she calmed down sheepishly wondering if she were getting baited into something.

"So what would be an acceptable reason for you to have a child?" Jared asked wrapping his arms around the shorter woman and drawing her closer to him until she was once again perched on his lap. Instead of answering, Ananda brushed her fingers across Jared's nipple enjoying the slight intake of breath that accompanied the motion. She seemed fascinated by the feel of it beneath her fingertips and continued the motion until Jared dipped down to take her mouth in a deep kiss once again. He could feel those fingertips dipping further down to sweep across his abs and the man couldn't help but take in a sharp breath as he went helpless with pleasure. He pressed deeper into the wet heat of Ananda's mouth and tried not to let the whimpers escape his mouth prematurely, instead burying one hand of his own into her soft hair and splaying the other across her back. They traded deeper kisses back and forth, tongues dueling and breaths co-mingling until Ananda pulled back with a small smile. Her hands moved up Jared's arms and across his shoulders.

"Do you like it when I touch you?"

"Yeah," Jared answered absently, the hand on her back moving down slowly until it cupped her hip in a tight grip. He lifted his gaze to Ananda's. "Do you want me to touch you?"

"Yes." Cupping Jared's cheek in her hand, Ananda brushed his stubbled cheekbone with her thumb and breathed deep as their scents once again wrapped around her. She would never be able to eat an orange without feeling a spike of arousal thanks to the man's heady scent. "God yes."

Slowly, Jared peeled Ananda out of her shirt, bending to kiss each inch of skin as it was revealed bit by bit. He turned them until her back was against the bed and repeated each step with her pants until she lay bare beneath him, her skin flushed with want and desire. Jared's hands slid down her sides until they pinned her hips against the bed. Keeping his eyes locked on hers, he shuffled down the bed until he could bury his nose in the dark hair above her core. The warm delicious smell curling about made his mouth water and he slowly tongued the edge of Ananda's folds, loving the little shiver that accompanied his moves. Ananda was lost as each pass of Jared's tongue sent waves of pleasure cascading over her heated body. She could feel herself tightening as her body pushed itself towards its first of many completions of the night. Ananda tried to fight it, tried to hold off her orgasm for as long as possible, but the feeling of Jared's tongue stabbing into her folds was the last piece of the puzzle that flung her head first into climax.

Coming back to, Ananda could see that Jared had divested himself of his own clothing and now knelt above her in all his naked glory. Reaching for her hand, he placed it on his shoulder before leaning down to drink from her lips again. "Touch me." The simple plea made Ananda quake with the need to have this man buried deep within her until she were unsure of where she began and he ended. Leaning up, Ananda kissed the small hollow in the center of Jared's chest before sliding her lips up until they connected with his once again. She broke the kiss in order to slip her lips once again down to Jared's sensitive nipple, capturing one in his mouth and flicking it with his tongue. Arching his back, Jared slid his hand into Ananda's hair, holding her in place until he was gasping at the sensations assaulting his body.

"You like that?" Ananda breathed out before switching to tend to the other pebbled nub.

"Yes," Jared answered with a shaky exhale. His breathing had sped up until it seemed loud in the otherwise quiet room.

"I want to touch you," Ananda confessed, cheeks heated and red. "I want to hold you and feel you moan and watch you come apart in my arms. And I want you to do the same to me until we're so lost in the feeling that we don't know what to do. I want to wreck you for anyone else and know that I'm the one who did that to you, who made you feel that and made you want so much. I want to ruin you for anyone else," Ananda said, tucking her face into the side of Jared's neck as her face heated up even more with embarrassment.

"Let's have a baby."

Chapter Two

Ananda's head shot up and she stared at Jared's totally serious face in confusion and wonder.

"What?"

Cupping Ananda's cheek, Jared smiled. "Ananda, I knew as soon as I saved you in that alley that I had found the one person I knew I could love. And that person is you. Yes everything is happening very quickly. Yes we are going to be on the run for a long while. Yes things will be a little dangerous, but I don't care. I don't care if this, if us, seems crazy. I know what I feel, and what I feel is a deep and never ending love for you. I want to be the one cheering you on and holding you tight. I want to see children with my dark hair and your beautiful eyes." Jared used his thumbs to wipe away the tears on Ananda's cheeks. "I love you and I always will, so having a baby with you is the logical next step. Not because it'll bring us closer or divert attention from us, but because our child will be a manifestation of our love for one another."

"Jared," Ananda whispered, her tears obscuring her vision as she reached up to hold the man's broad shoulders. "I love you too."

Once again their lips met, but this time there was no softness; the tenderness had been replaced with blinding need and passion as they writhed against one another.

Ananda reveled in feeling the hard planes of Jared's muscular body and she opened her knees enough for the man to slip between them, the hardness of his engorged cock pushing slightly against Ananda. She whimpered as she felt her body pump out slick in order to ease the way for their joining. Jared groaned as the scent of their arousal grew stronger.

"Kerri!"

Ananda and Jared froze at Ryan's loud shout, both torn between laughter and fear that all was not as it seemed mere moments ago. The sound of twin groans of pleasure leaking from the other side of the wall put them firmly in the category of uncontrollable laughter and they collapsed against one another, nakedness forgotten in their amusement.

Tears fell from Ananda's eyes as she struggled to overcome feelings of happiness that her friend and brother were happy and disgust at hearing anything remotely sexual coming from her brother. Opening her eyes she was treated to the breathtaking sight of Jared caught helpless in the throes of glee, his handsome face split wide by his large smile. Right then and there she swore to do whatever she could to make him smile like that again and again no matter what the cost. She untangled one hand from the man's thick mane and gently cradled his cheek bringing his attention back to their current state of arousal and undress. Jared leaned down to once again take Ananda's lips in a passionate yet tender kiss.

"How about we get them back with a few noises of our own?" Ananda whispered, the smile on her face as wide as ever.

"Sounds like more than a good enough idea for me. What did you have in mind?" Jared was unsure of what exactly the woman may have planned, but he had a feeling that whatever it was he would enjoy it greatly. He tried to probe Ananda's mind a little to see if he could glean any details that would prepare him for it, but all he got were vague feelings and the mental picture of a middle finger. Refocusing, he looked down to see Ananda smiling sharply, her gaze predatory in a way he never thought he would see.

"Are you trying to read my mind sir?" Ananda asked, hands moving down until they were grazing Jared's abs. He couldn't help the shiver that crawled up his spine and he could feel his heartbeat pick up at Ananda's new boldness. He found himself enjoying her taking the lead and him following which was something that had never occurred to him before. Perhaps this would open up a lot more doors in terms of their sexual relationship and he wondered how it might change things once Ananda felt more comfortable with her own assertiveness. Jared shivered again as he thought of the things Ananda might eventually ask for or try behind closed doors.

"Well I was, but I realized that I might prefer being surprised by your newfound boldness," Jared answered.

Ananda smiled at Jared's answer before pushing the man up and away. Her body protested the lack of contact, but she ignored it in favor of turning over and baring her naked back to him. The look she threw over her shoulder made Jared's body tighten with want and his gaze flowed from the back of her flushed neck down to where her thighs met. He could see her lips glistening and his mouth watered with the desire to taste her deeply.

"I thought we could possibly do something a bit different than before," Ananda said. She hesitated for a moment before leaning down, her shoulders resting on the bed, as she grasped her butt cheeks pulling them apart. "I've…you know I'm not a virgin, but I've never tried…this…here. God, I'm not doing this very well, but you get what I mean right?"

Jared was floored. It wouldn't be the first time he had ever tried anal, but the fact that Ananda was offering somehow hit him harder. Shakily he leaned in and skimmed his fingers up and down the edge of her puckered hole. "It will hurt a little…" he trailed off trying to be honest despite how much his body wanted.

Smiling, Ananda reached back and put the man's finger against her hole. "I know, but I want this. I want you everywhere inside me." She rested her cheek down on the pillow and gazed at Jared adoringly. She was aware that the first time would hurt, but she wasn't afraid. Ananda knew that Jared would take care of her and she was excited to offer this first to him.

Rocking back on his heels, Jared took a deep breath to center himself and prepare. "Alright. Just relax for me okay? I want this to be as painless as possible for you." He slid his finger into the pulsing warmth of Ananda's vagina, scooping as much of her gathering wetness and transferring it to her virginal opening. He could feel her inhale deeply as he slowly pushed one finger in, the tightness intoxicating.

"You alright baby?"

Ananda sighed relaxing her body even more and practically melting into the bed. "Yes, keep going." Ananda could tell that Jared was being as sweet and caring as possible when it came to preparing her for this addition to their sex life. She would occasionally tense up only to relax once again when the man would massage her lower back or kiss her inner thigh until all she could feel was pleasure. "I'm ready baby please!"

"Okay," Jared groaned, body twitching slightly with his need. He had been trying hard to do his best to make Ananda's body ready but now he was worried that he'd come immediately upon entering her hot virgin hole. He readjusted himself, right arm holding him prone above her body and left hand wrapped around his cock to guide it into Ananda's opening. The first breach of his head into her hole made him grit his teeth and he paused to give her and himself time to cope before pushing in again. By the time his hips touched hers, they were both groaning with pleasure. "You okay baby?"

"Jared," Ananda groaned. "I know you are worried about me, but if you ask again instead of moving I will find someone else to give me what I want. Move!"

Jared was surprised by Ananda's outburst but did as ordered, slowly pulling back in order to thrust in again. With each pleasured gasp of the woman underneath him, he moved a little bit faster until the bed was creaking and banging against the wall with the force of their thrusts. Their voices blended together as they vocalized their pleasure to the world. Jared tangled their fingers together until with one final shout, they came together, backs arched and thoughts mingled together radiating pleasure and love.

<<◇>>

Packing up their meager belongings was proving bittersweet for Ananda as she thought of everything that had transpired over the last four days. Somehow everything she had ever known about her life, her future and herself had changed. The thought of what could have been, graduating college, getting married, having a career and starting a family, almost threatened to consume her in a haze of panic and overwhelming emotion.

"Ana, are you okay?" The rough baritone of Jared's voice cut a path through the swirl of her thoughts and Ananda felt herself calm at the warmth of the man's hand as it brushed lightly down her arm. His scent enveloped her in a sea of strength as she truly took stock of what she had: her brother and best friend, happy together and joining them on their journey to escape and secure a better life that promised continuous freedom, a better understanding of who she was and what her gifts could do…and love. No matter how much the thoughts of what could have been tried to overwhelm her, Ananda could not help but be grateful for that one night that changed everything, the night that brought Jared to her. She gazed up into the eyes of the man she knew without a shadow of a doubt that she would love and cherish for the rest of her life.

"I am now."

Smiling, Jared leaned down to brush his lips against Ananda's forehead before stooping slightly to grab their bags. With a final glance around, the man turned and exited the room walking swiftly to the waiting car as if he somehow knew that Ananda needed a moment to herself to cross that final threshold into what would become her new life.

Ananda gazed at the woman in the mirror, her short, pixie-cut blond hair, startlingly bright in the waning evening light. She could almost swear that it was someone else staring back at her if not for the golden eyes that gazed back with a new fearlessness that seemed to glow from within. No matter what happened, Ananda knew she would be okay.

After all, if trouble tried to find her she would see it before it even came.

-The End-

If you enjoyed this series, I would appreciate your leaving a review of the book. Good reviews encourage an author to write as well as help books to sell. Good reviews can be just a few short sentences describing what you liked about the book without having a spoiler. If you could spend 30 seconds writing a review, I would appreciate it: you can review this title right now at your favorite retailer.

Here is a preview of **another story** you may enjoy:

Valtina's Redemption - The Leather Satchel Paranormal Romance Series, Book 1

NOT EVERYONE was given a second chance, especially after failing so many times before. Valtina was among the lucky few who got a real opportunity to redeem themselves. She was a spirit trapped in The Middle World: a place filled with souls who have gone astray and were not granted entrance into The Afterlife until they have learned a few lessons and found their place. These were lost souls in a way, and Valtina was most likely just a lifetime away from discovering her true identity. Right now, however, she was summoned by Ladaya to discuss a task that may grant her access to The Afterlife if she can complete it successfully. Valtina waited hopefully for her to arrive.

Ladaya has already perfected her soul. She has earned her place in The Afterlife, but she has also learned what it means to help others, and so she returned regularly to guide souls through their journey and to help them succeed on their own paths. Now, she coalesced out of the gray fog surrounding them. Valtina's face lit up with excitement and a hint of nervousness. Thoughts flooded her mind of the different jobs she may be asked to complete, and she was worried that they may not be things she herself can do. Nevertheless, she held her composure, hopeful that she might be reunited with her family and lovers in The Afterlife.

"Hello, Valtina," Ladaya smiled warmly at her.

"Hello."

"Thank you for agreeing to meet me today… I really need your help. If you can do this successfully, I'll reward you in the fullest. It will be worth it in more ways than one, trust me."

"I'm happy to help, but what exactly do you want me to do?"

"Given the grave matter we are dealing with, I am going to need to leave a lot of the decision making to you. But I'll give you a bit of background information to get you started. As you may have noticed in your last life, the world is on a decline, especially in the area of love. Couples are no longer able to love each other the way that they should. Cheating is becoming a normal thing—many partners are having extramarital affairs and sleeping with multiple women while trying to keep up the appearance that they are 'dedicated' to their wives or girlfriend. Even more couples are only staying together because of lust, and no other attraction towards the other person. They don't love each other and their relationships are meaningless.

"This might not seem like a huge problem at first, but the entire universe is based on love and human compassion. That's something that we can't survive without, and evil is tempting people away from their core values. It won't take long before the world is in tatters and everything will fall apart. Now, this is where you come in."

"I'm going to need you to help breathe life and passion back into relationships that have gone stale and started to fall apart. Over the centuries, I've seen how you are in each life that you have lived. You are dripping with sexual energy and you have had some of the most successful relationships that I've ever seen. I know that you can do this job. I need you to do this for me."

Valtina pondered this for a few moments, doubting whether or not she would be able to successfully do the task expected of her. Even though she may have been able to understand everything in the world, she had always been successful in her love life, in every life. She felt confident with the idea that she won't have to save any lives or stop a bombing or anything complicated like that. She smiled as she realized that this could actually be a fun thing for her and she was practically beaming as she started to speak, "Alright, I'll do it. Where should I start?"

"Well, to begin with, there's a couple that we know who are truly meant to be together. Their names are Samantha and Joshua. They recently got married—only 4 years ago. Already, their sex lives are deteriorating. I want you to fix this. They haven't been intimate in months. Although I'm not entirely sure why this is, I know that they both would be interested in trying some light bondage and they'll be much better off with a change of pace."

She smiled more, realizing that she would be in her element throughout this job. "Sounds good… I can do that, no problem."

"For you to use, I want you to take this leather satchel. It contains some of the most important things that will help you work with these couples. I'm also going to give you some basic abilities that will help you read their minds or redirect their thoughts; inspire them though, don't take control."

"Sure thing."

"I believe in you, Valtina. I know that you will save us."

<<◇>>

Valtina dissolved into the fog and reappeared in a modest apartment. The room was filled with photographs and cozy-looking furniture. In an armchair, Joshua was sitting on his own while his wife was curled up on the couch at the other side of the living room. Valtina stood there taking in the scene, saddened to see a married couple sitting apart when they would obviously be more comfortable sitting together.

A few moments after Valtina got there, as she continued taking in her surroundings, the man stood up and stretched. He yawned, "Honey, I'm going to bed. Are you coming with me?"

It took a moment for Samantha to answer. She was zoned out, staring blankly at the television. "Oh, no, not right now. I think I'm going to read for a while and take a shower first. Have a good night." As she talked, she leaned forward and opened up a book from the coffee table.

"Alright, have a good night. I love you."

She didn't answer; she was already pretending to be absorbed in the words on the page in front of her. Even Joshua knew that she heard but chose to ignore him. Valtina was already starting to worry that this job might be harder than she expected as she watched Joshua walk slowly to the bedroom and Samantha sit on the couch, resolved to making him miserable and prolonging her misery. This brief scene was an obvious representation of the heartache that was here.

It was clear that all Joshua wanted was to be closer to this wife, and that was understandable. After all, who wouldn't? With the abilities that Valtina had, she knew that he had been trying for months to improve things with her, but Samantha wasn't willing to do anything else. She was bored and it was clear that things needed to change.

Valtina understood both sides of the situation. Joshua loved his wife and he wanted to make her happy, but he clearly didn't know how. Samantha still loved her husband, but after doing the exact same thing for so long, it was hard to be passionate about vanilla sex. As she considered this, Valtina decided that she will have to start work first thing in the morning.

If you enjoyed this sample then look for **Valtina's Redemption - The Leather Satchel Paranormal Romance Series, Book 1**.

Here is a preview of **another story** you may enjoy:

The Awakening: The Daemon Paranormal Romance Chronicles, Book 1

THE LAST customer of the day was slowly leaving. Phoebe reached down to pet her dog, Ace, and moved to close up shop. Since graduating high school, she had worked in fairs across the country as a fortune teller, saving money. She did not know why, but when she touched somebody's hand, she could read their thoughts. Although she could not divine their future, she could make educated guesses that were enough to bring customers back. After saving enough money, she had finally opened up her own shop.

Removing the scarf from around her hair, Phoebe let her red curls cascade along her shoulders. Ace sniffed at some of his dog food while she reached over to grab her purse. Before she could close up, a knock at the door surprised her. In front of the door, she saw one of the most gorgeous men she had ever laid eyes on. Curious, she opened the door and let him in.

"Hello! How can I help you, Mr...?" She paused and waited for him to respond.

"My name is Apollo Mikos. Pleasure to meet you, Phoebe Williams." The blonde-haired man reached for her hand and shook it. Instantly, a vision arose before her eyes of Apollo and her rolling around in bed sheets. Waves crashed outside the window—a storm was brewing. As the vision of Apollo entered her body forcefully, Phoebe pulled her hand back. The vision went away, but it left a slight blush on Phoebe's cheeks. Reading the minds of other people was occasionally embarrassing and often felt like a major invasion of privacy. Still, she found herself wishing that she could have held his hand a little longer to see where these thoughts took her.

Motioning toward the table and chairs reserved for clients, she asked if he wanted to sit down. Apollo just shook his head.

"I need your help with something, but not like that." He shrugged his shoulders. Tall and well-built, Apollo had blue eyes and chiseled features. He wore a dark black suit that made all of his muscles ripple beneath the fabric.

Confused, Phoebe looked over at him. "What do you mean?"

Sighing, Apollo looked into her eyes. "You will probably want to sit down for this." Still uncertain, Phoebe sat down and waited for him to speak again.

Gazing out the window, Apollo framed his thoughts. "I know your mother, Rhea. I also know what you really are and I need your help."

Phoebe was aghast. "What do you mean? I don't have a mother. I grew up in foster care after my mother left me there when I was two."

If you enjoyed this sample then look for **The Awakening: The Daemon Paranormal Romance Chronicles, Book 1**.

Here is a preview of **another story** you may enjoy:

Alpha Packed: A BBW Paranormal Shifter Romance - Book 1

THIS WAS a huge mistake. Darlene should have known better, but in utter and total desperation, she agreed to this date. Now the guy in front of her—what was his name again? Steve? Mike? She couldn't even remember now—had been talking non-stop about pro wrestling. But not even actual real wrestling. The stuff that was fake and basically just soap operas with some terrible phony fights thrown in.

"So then the Ice Cube challenged The Man to a battle!"

"Wow, really?" Darlene replied, feigning interest on every possible level.

This was her mistake. She had been spending way too much time at home lately, curled up on the couch, binge watching reality television shows because they made her feel better about her boring life. Darlene would leave for work in the mornings, do eight hours at a boring local bookstore, come home, eat and watch TV. She also stayed up far later than any normal human should, which resulted in limited forms of social communication.

That was how Darlene ended up on some free dating website. She deleted most of the messages she got. They were mostly from guys who seemed to think of her as a sexual fetish instead of an actual human being. Getting messages from guys who were into her being overweight made her feel uncomfortable. Darlene either got disgusted looks or sexual lust over her size. Both sucked. She had been about to delete her page for good when a guy who appeared to be normal messaged her. He hadn't made any gross comments about her size and even made her laugh once or twice with his messages. It had been eight months since her last relationship blew up in her face. *Why not try something different?* She decided to accept his date.

The guy was so boring that Darlene wished the restaurant would go up in flames so she could flee. She was flipping through her options on how to end the date early when he finally pushed his plate away.

"That was delicious," he said.

"Oh yeah. It was great," Darlene lied, thinking the potatoes were too dry for her liking.

The check came and the guy—what was his name!—made an effort to search for his wallet. *Oh here we go...*

"Oh man. I forgot my wallet at home!" he said with fake surprise.

"Yeah, yeah, I got it," she mumbled, slamming her debit card on the table.

It didn't take a genius to figure out this asshole had asked her out to throw her what he thought was a "pity date" and get a free meal out of her. He would probably go home to all his idiot friends and talk about how he gave the fat girl a date because he was just so nice. Darlene felt like punching him in the face.

She paid, and they walked out of the restaurant in silence. He escorted her to her car and then glanced around, as if checking so that no one could see him, before he tried to kiss her.

"Yeah," Darlene lifted up her hand to block him, "I don't think so. Thanks for nothing though, seriously."

The man scowled and before he could say something back, Darlene got into her car. She pulled out of the parking lot as quickly as she could, wanting to forget the entire terrible date.

What a mistake. What an absolute mistake. Not even just the date. The last couple years of her life had been a huge mistake. She wished she could travel back in time and re-do everything. The first thing she'd do would be to say a resounding *no* when Austin proposed to her.

Darlene pulled into her apartment complex five minutes later. She had picked a nearby restaurant so she could make a quick escape home if needed. She walked up to the second floor. The couple by the stairwell was fighting again. They were constantly screaming at each other over everything. Some nights, Darlene wanted to yell back at them to just break up. Other times, she wanted to tell them to make it work, because being alone was terrible.

She opened the front door of her apartment and glanced around. Her computer was on in one corner, and a few blankets were thrown on the couch for maximum comfort for those times when she drowned herself in ice cream and terrible reality shows. Everything else was clean though. Darlene couldn't stand her apartment being messy or dirty. She wanted it to be perfect, as if she could make her apartment look like how she didn't feel.

Darlene yanked off her high heels and plopped down in front of her computer. She deleted the online dating profile and stared out the window. That was it — she was going to become a hermit. Well, as much of a hermit as one can be if they still had to go to work and grocery shop and run errands…but other than that she was totally going to be a hermit from now on. People were not her thing. People were just terrible all around. And she'd had enough of terrible people.

She moved to the couch, wrapping herself up in a blanket. Darlene mused over what she would watch. Terrible shows about being tricked into online dating seemed like a good end to the night. It'd make her feel better at the very least.

Her cellphone rang loudly. Darlene jolted awake, startled. She wasn't used to her new ringtone. It used to be the theme song of an old cartoon she liked, but after everything went to hell she changed it to a normal ring in an effort to seem more adult. Now the ring was bleating loudly and annoying her. She looked at the front of the screen… her boss.

"Hello?"

"Hey, sorry, did I wake you?"

"No, Maria," Darlene lied. "What's up?"

"I had to fire Jacob. Can you cover his shift? You'd be working till three."

Darlene glanced at the clock to see it was a little past eight in the morning. "That's fine. I'll leave now."

She hopped in the shower, letting the warm water rush over her. She wasn't surprised that Maria had to fire Jacob. He was constantly late and unable to help any of the customers who came into the shop. The bookstore was small and dealt with books that couldn't be found at any of the chains. Business was slow, but the books were rare enough that Maria only needed to sell a few each month to keep the business going. Darlene liked how quiet it was and the fact that human interaction was minimal. She knew she needed to get over this slump she was in, but felt no desire to. Almost everything Darlene did as of late seemed to feed into it — her lifestyle, her job, even the stupid things she spent time watching and looking up online.

The bookstore was only a ten-minute drive to downtown and located between a coffee shop and a cheesy massage parlor. Maria hated the massage parlor. She thought it was tacky and ruined the charm of the street. Darlene usually liked to watch to see how many guys went in there. She swore it was a front for some hookers.

Darlene parked her car and headed toward the bookshop. She could already tell no one was in the store. She walked inside and waved to Maria.

"Oh, I am so glad you are here!" Maria exclaimed when she saw Darlene. "I'll have to hire someone right away, but you and I will have to work extra in the meantime."

"No problem," Darlene replied, shoving her purse under the front counter.

Darlene worked here for almost four years. Maria was a good boss. She always treated Darlene with respect and even gave her an entire month off after her father passed away three years ago. She was an older Native American woman with a bushy head of white hair that she barely cared enough to run a comb through. She wore large glasses that looked like they were from the seventies. Her fashion left a lot to be desired. Maria seemed to put on whatever she grabbed first and didn't look twice in the mirror afterward. For instance, today she had on a blue shirt with an off-color green skirt and black shoes. Her earrings were painted octopuses she had probably made herself — she liked making crazy jewelry.

"So," Darlene asked. "What happened with Jacob?"

Maria scowled. "He comes into work high as a kite, stinking of weed. Starts rambling to me about how he was in the woods last night and *like, totally felt something, like, man*," Maria said, mimicking Jacob's slow tone. "He was an hour late on top of it. I can't have someone late, stinking of weed and scaring off the few customers I get each month… especially after the last incident."

"Yeah, that was a mess." Jacob had hit on one of their regular clients in such a crass manner that she had threatened never to return again.

"Anyway, thank you so much for covering. I'm going to head off now. One of the grandkids is having a birthday party. You'll be okay?"

Darlene cast a sarcastic glance around the empty bookstore. "Wow, I hope I can handle it."

Maria laughed and grabbed her purse, heading to the door before stopping. "Hey, how was your date?"

Darlene frowned. "A total mess."

"Sorry, love. Hang in there, okay?" Maria said before leaving.

Hang in there. Darlene sighed. She has been hanging in there for way too long. When was she going to get a grip on her own life again? She walked around the shop to make sure everything was in its proper place. Darlene knew it would be, of course. It wasn't as if they had a ton of customers come through.

Maria had the marketable books up front, which brought in some tourist traffic during the summer. The farther back in the store one went, the stranger the books became. Darlene ended up in the back again, like she always did. Maria kept the supernatural books back here — books about ghosts, werewolves, mermaids and all sorts of paranormal creatures. Darlene always felt drawn to these; she never knew why. As a kid, she liked to pretend to be a ghost hunter. Nowadays, she liked to watch terrible B-movies about ghosts.

She trailed her fingers along the spines, letting the musty old-book smell wash over her. Darlene stopped in front of one book about ghosts, pulling it off the shelf. She had just flipped it open to a random page when the tiny bell on the door jingled. Surprised, Darlene looked up.

A tall man in amazing shape walked in. He had brown eyes, a beard and scruffy hair and wore a leather jacket. Darlene found herself gawking at him. He was so handsome her knees turned to jelly.

"Hi!" she said, but her voice sounded too high pitched, like she was eleven. "Hi, sorry, back here." She walked up front to him.

"Hello," he said in a deep voice that sent shivers down her back.

"Hi," Darlene repeated and then tried to get a hold of herself. "How can I help you?"

"I'm lost. I'm trying to find Roman's Tavern."

Her eyes widened. "I don't know if it's open yet."

Was this guy a hardcore alcoholic? It was still early in the morning, and he wanted to find a bar. Roman's Tavern was the only bar in town that Darlene hadn't ever gone to. It brought in a wild crowd that made her uneasy. Any time she drove past it and saw the crazy partying in there, she realized how much she wanted to go and that scared her. She was never much of a partier. The fact that such an overwhelming urge to go when she drove by made her nervous. What if she went and lost her head?

The cops were there often, breaking up fights. Bike gangs were always seen there. Sometimes, if she left work at closing time, she'd drive by it and hear the thumping music and smell the cigarette smoke. She thought about going in every time. What would happen?

Would she get hurt? What if she was missing out on something?

To Darlene, Roman's Tavern represented a life she could jump into if only she wasn't afraid. But she *was* too afraid. Life as a hermit was too comforting.

"Do you know where I can find it anyway?" he asked.

"It's down the street. On the corner, kind of pushed back a bit. It has this rundown broken sign that you might see if you drive by it."

"Thanks a lot, Miss…"

"Darlene." She held out her hand.

He stared at it for a second and then shook it. "Idris. Thanks for the help. You guys sell books about ghosts?" He pointed to the book she was holding when he came in.

His hand was so warm that Darlene had to snap herself back to the conversation. Was he sick? Shouldn't he be resting instead of going to some bar?

"Yes," she managed to respond. "We have a supernatural section in the back. Ghosts, vampires, werewolves…the usual."

"Werewolves, huh?" he replied. "Okay, well, nice to meet you."

Before Darlene could say anything else, he was gone.

She stood there, clutching her book to her chest, thinking about the feeling of warmth from his hand. What in the world was that about?

If you enjoyed this sample then look for **Alpha Packed: A BBW Paranormal Shifter Romance - Book 1**.

Here is a preview of **another story** you may also enjoy:

Devil's Advocate: A BBW MC New Adult Romance Series - Book 1 by Carla Coxwell

KRISTIE LOOKED at the sky as she pulled up in front of the casino. The air was chilly and the clouds were dark and threatening snow, which was the last thing Kristie felt like dealing with. She had been in her car for over ten hours, driving home from college for the holidays. Her back was sore and her legs needed to be stretched out. She wanted a hot bath in a Jacuzzi tub. She'd settle for a hot tub. But who was she kidding? There was no hot tub to be found at her parents' house and trying to have a hot bath without being interrupted was almost impossible.

Kristie had approached the holidays with an ever-growing sense of dread. It wasn't that she didn't want to see her mother, but every time she came home, it was like being suffocated. Her hometown had held more appeal for her when she was younger, back when her father was alive. Since he'd died and her mother had gotten remarried last year, Kristie had delayed going home at all. She had only met her step-father in passing and hadn't met his nephew, who he tried to raise on his own.

Kristie had saved up to stay at a hotel the entire break. It had made the most sense to her. It would cause the least amount of stress during her stay and give her space when she needed it. But when she had mentioned this to her mother, there was no way to mistake the sadness in her mother's voice for anything else. Knowing she was upsetting her mother by refusing to stay at home with her new family, Kristie had cancelled the reservation and agreed to stay at her mother's house instead.

She looked up at the casino where her mother had worked the last five years. Her mother worked in the back offices, far away from the lights from the slot machines and the sounds of people winning money. The casino was a little run down but brought in a steady stream of people who could afford the middle-level slots and risks it provided in a town that was mostly quiet.

The stale smell of cigarettes and alcohol hit Kristie in the face as she stepped inside. She looked around, seeing if anything had changed since the last time she had been here. Nothing jumped out of her. A few of the slots seemed to have been upgraded, but the carpet was still worn down and dirty and the place had an air of despair that made Kristie's skin crawl. She had never been to Las Vegas, but she imagined that the casinos there weren't as depressing.

Kristie made her way to the back and asked for her mother through the grate where an attendant was standing, looking at her cellphone. The woman went off to find her mother, and Kristie was soon ushered into the back offices. The casino décor quickly ended back here. Her mother's small office was near the back, shoved in a corner. The door was ajar, and Kristie peeked her head in.

Her mother was looking at the computer, squinting through her glasses to whatever was on the screen. When Kristie knocked on the door gently, her mother looked up and smiled. Kristie was startled to see she was going gray. The last time she had seen her mother, she had been a brunette. It was odd to see age creeping up on her. She came over to her and hugged her tightly.

"It's so nice to see you again."

"You, too, Mom."

Her mom urged her to sit down as she sat across from her at her desk. It made Kristie feel odd, as if she was interviewing to be her mother's daughter. Her mom didn't seem to notice, however, and smiled again. They made small talk for a while, mostly talking about Kristie's experiences at college. Kristie felt tired. She knew her mom meant well, but she really wanted to go home and nap. She was only here to get the address to her mom's new place.

"How are things with Lionel?" Kristie finally asked, feeling as if she didn't bring up her mom's new husband, she would never get out of the tiny office.

Her mom seemed to relax now that Kristie had brought him up, "He's great. Really, we're just wonderful. There are some issues, though…"

"Like what?"

"Well, it's actually one of the reasons that we wanted you to stay with us instead of a hotel. See, Lionel's nephew, Gray, is a bit of a handful. Lionel still feels responsible for him since he became his legal guardian when Gray was just a little boy."

Kristie wasn't following, "Okay…"

"He tends to run on the wrong side of the law, and we thought it'd be so great if you two could meet and maybe hang out."

The words hung in the air. Kristie felt a twinge of annoyance. She had thought her mother wanted her at the house because she had missed her, not because she wanted her to play nice with her new step-father's nephew. They weren't in grade school anymore. Trying to change someone set in their ways by sticking them with a goody-goody was a useless attempt.

Kristie took a deep breath and held it for a few seconds, letting the air out slowly. Her mother watched, a worried expression on her face.

"What do you want me to do with him?" Kristie finally asked.

Her mom, taking the fact that Kristie hadn't said no as a good sign, started to ramble. "Well, maybe just hang out with him. Show him what you do for fun. Maybe you two can go to the movies or something."

Kristie raised an eyebrow, "Go to the movies? What does this guy do for fun anyway that has you two so stressed out?"

Her mom avoided her stare and sighed, looking tired. "He runs with a bad crowd and doesn't like to listen. He's a good kid though. He's just lost."

"And you think I can fix him?"

"It wouldn't hurt to try, would it, Kristie? For me?"

Kristie sighed and nodded in agreement. How could she say no to her mother? She would always wish that her mother hadn't gotten remarried, but she didn't want her mom to be unhappy either. Her mom got up and walked over to her, hugging her tightly. Her mother's hugs had always reminded Kristie of being a little kid, outside playing till the sun set and running back inside for dinner. Back when her father was alive. Kristie shut her eyes tightly, willing the memories to leave her. She didn't want to think about her father right now.

Her mom finally pulled away and looked at her, smiling, "We'll have to really talk, you know, all about college and everything."

"Yeah, of course."

Her mom's eyes swept down her quickly, so fast that if Kristie wasn't used to it, she never would have picked up on it. She steeled herself.

"Maybe you and Gray can go to the gym. It'd get him out of the house and you could lose a few pounds at the same time," her mom said cheerfully.

Kristie mumbled in agreement and gave her mother one last hug before leaving the office. She should have known that there wasn't going to be any way in hell that her mother would have let an entire conversation go without making some sort of remark to her about her weight.

As she trudged through the casino, her mood lowered with every step. She regretted coming here for the holidays. Before her, they spread out in a bleak landscape. Dealing with her mother's 'helpful advice' in regards to her weight, and trying to show her loser relative by marriage around town. At the very least, she should have kept the hotel reservation.

Kristie dragged out the drive toward Lionel's house. Her mother had given her the address and it was close to the casino. A ten-minute drive didn't seem like enough time to prepare for whatever she was going to walk into. As she turned down the street where her mom's new house was, she found herself taking a deep breath. The first time, she just drove past the house. It was non-descript and had nothing of worth showing that made Kristie even notice it. Her mom had stopped gardening after her father died, and the front yard of this house was plain and dull.

Kristie pulled into the driveway. The garage door was open and a man was underneath a truck, working on it. She could only see his feet. Kristie got out of her car, grabbing her bags, and looked inside the garage. The man didn't look up when she shut the door of her car.

"Hello?" Kristie called out toward the man under the truck.

He didn't answer. Heavy metal was blasting out of a stereo nearby, but it was such an old stereo that the music sounded tinny. Kristie called out again, but the man still didn't answer. She knew that he heard her because he stopped working at one point and went still before resuming. She hoped this wasn't Lionel, because the guy was an asshole. *Probably his fantastic nephew.* Kristie trudged toward the front door, leaving the other guy behind. What a fantastic trip this was going to be.

If you enjoyed this sample then look for **Devil's Advocate: A BBW MC New Adult Romance Series - Book 1 by Carla Coxwell**.

Other Books by Darla Dunbar

- The Romeo Alpha BBW Paranormal Shifter Romance Series

- Romeo Alpha Blood Lines Romance Series

- The Alpha Feud BBW Paranormal Shifter Romance Series

- The Alpha Packed BBW Paranormal Shifter Romance Series

- The Daemon Paranormal Romance Chronicles

- The Leather Satchel Paranormal Romance Series

Get the latest update on new releases from the author at:

https://darladunbar.com/newsletter/

About the Author - Darla Dunbar

Darla has been interested in paranormal romance since she was a teenager in high school. It was then that she discovered she could fulfill her fantasies through her writing.

Observing people and human behavior in the area of romance has always been one of her favorite pastimes. Combining that with an overactive imagination is a sure fire way of coming up with interesting themes.

Connect with Darla Dunbar

I really appreciate you reading my book! Here are my social media coordinates:

Friend me on Facebook:
https://www.facebook.com/darladunbar/

Follow me on Twitter: https://twitter.com/DarlDunbar

Check me out on Goodreads:
https://www.goodreads.com/author/show/8425857.Darl a_Dunbar

Subscribe to my newsletter:
https://darladunbar.com/newsletter/

Visit my website: https://darladunbar.com/